The Earth Trembled,
The Mounts Rushed To Meet....

Now Loadice was a young and agile knight. He gained his feet some time before Raum and ran toward the dark knight with sword drawn. Raum's big hand had just touched the hilt of his sword when it was struck by a stinging blow. His other arm, however, was raised high, ax in hand.

Before Loadice could recover his stance, the ax fell with lightning speed and all could hear the metal of his bright helmet tear asunder, followed by the death cry of the brave Loadice.

Raum hacked the young knight's head from its body and threw it, blood streaming, at the feet of Arthur.

All about the field stood in horror and drew blades to avenge this outrage.

RAUM

BY CARL SHERRELL

AVON
PUBLISHERS OF BARD, CAMELOT AND DISCUS BOOKS

RAUM is an original publication of Avon Books. This work has never before appeared in book form.

AVON BOOKS
A division of
The Hearst Corporation
959 Eighth Avenue
New York, New York 10019

First Avon Printing, May, 1977

AVON TRADEMARK REG. U.S. PAT. OFF. AND IN
OTHER COUNTRIES, MARCA REGISTRADA, HECHO EN
U.S.A.

Printed in the U.S.A.

*I wish to dedicate this book
to my three elven ladies,
Carol, Lee and Lynn.*

Raum

PART 1

Upon Entering the World

FAR TO THE NORTH in what was once ancient Thule dwelt a very ambitious sorcerer whom we shall call Jord since his real name would be unpronounceable by most today. This dealer in magic and incantations was quite adept, make no mistake, inheriting much knowledge of his craft from his great-great-great-grandfather who lived before the rise to power of the Mabden, or mankind as they are now termed. The rulers of those days in Thule were gods and giants from races that have long vanished from the earth just as the islands that gave them birth now rest beneath the great sea. I mention this historical note only to assure you that Jord's incantations were of a very authentic and high quality. It was not the magic that was faulty that fateful night, but Jord's damnable curiosity and flair for the romantic.

Now, to be sure, it was Asteroth summoned by Jord, although by a different name. His circled design had been well drawn, small fires burning at each point of the pentagram. The incantations were clearly said. Thus it was that Jord was understandably surprised when the figure that stepped forth from the boiling smoke was obviously not that of the desired demon.

The creature shook its black plumage, for at first it most resembled a giant raven, but after a moment seemed more like a huge, blue-black warrior in sooty armor. His taloned left hand rested on the hilt of a heavy broadsword that hung at his side. His right arm, thick with muscle, carried his massive ebony shield which bore a strange emblem of brass inlay. From the dark warrior's open visor shone two terrifying red eyes.

"But who . . . what . . ." stammered the startled magician.

"I come in Lord Asteroth's stead," boomed the awful voice.

"Why is this?" demanded Jord petulantly, suddenly replacing his fear with curiosity.

"He has a very important council at the moment," replied the knight. "What task may I perform for you before I depart?"

"That seems of little import now," stated Jord, becoming intrigued with his guest. "By what name are you called?"

"Raum," boomed the giant's voice.

"What is your title and station?" asked Jord. "I've never heard of you."

"Few have ever summoned me. I am only an earl among the Fallen Ones."

"But what tasks do you perform best?"

"I see the past and future as clearly as the present. I crush cities and cause quakes. I also cause love between parties even if they be enemies."

"Love!" cried Jord in disbelief. "I beg your lordship's pardon but I find it difficult to cast one such as yourself as the bringer of love. Death seems more fitting."

"You see me very well," said the Knight removing

his black-winged helmet. His head was wide and seemed chiseled from dark stone. The red eyes shone from beneath heavy brows. His nose was short and decidedly arched. His upper lip was massive and curled in an evil smile revealing yellow fangs.

"I was the bringer of love to the old races. Their vision of love was quite different from that held now among you Mabden."

"No doubt you speak the truth," shuddered Jord, "but, my Lord Raum, you mentioned departing from here. I must remind you of the rules, I fear, since you have had little experience in such things for a few thousands of years."

"Of what rules do you speak?" hissed the towering presence.

"I speak of the rule that you go nowhere until I say you might since it is only with my permission that you are here at all. Now where did you think you were going, back to the Netherworld?"

"I go into the world to find one who may help me."

"Help you?" laughed Jord. "You do not appear to be in need of assistance. Who is this man you feel can help a god . . . a fallen god I grant you, but a god none the less?"

"He is in the isles where the one called Arthur rules. His name is Merlin."

"That Druid?" exclaimed Jord. "What could that old trickster do for you that I could not?"

"There is a new thought and understanding at Arthur's court. You or your people do not have this new thought. Merlin is this court's magician. He can answer my questions."

"But if you perceive events yet to come," insisted Jord, "why must you ask questions?"

"To see is not always to understand," retorted Raum.

"For what reason do you appear in your black armor?"

"I see this court of the Round Table occupied by men of arms. This is how I shall present myself."

"Ah!" cried Jord, exploding into peals of uncontrolled laughter.

"Silence!" The black knight's voice stopped all sound in the frightened sorcerer's throat. After a moment Jord gathered his courage once more.

"You forget," stated Jord, "I give orders on this plane. Now relax the grip on your blade and I shall explain my laughter. You see, my innocent . . . if that be the proper word for your case, you could never just stride into Arthur's famed court at Camelot with your . . . appearance. All would set upon you for what you are, a devil."

"But I mean them no harm."

"I fear you would have little opportunity to explain," said Jord shaking his gray head. "Can you not see this in your future?"

"This is one of the great mysteries in which Merlin may aid me. I can see nothing of my own future."

"Ah then, my friend, I would say you possess an altogether worthless gift," frowned Jord.

"Will you release me from your circled charm, then?" demanded Raum.

"Not quite yet," replied Jord confidently, his little wicked eyes dancing. "I am beginning to see how we may be of assistance to one another. How may I trust your word if you give it?"

"I would give my word as a noble."

"Ah, yes," laughed Jord, "but you are a noble of what kingdom? I shouldn't say it is one devoted to truth and fairness."

"You will trust me anyway," growled Raum. "Let us be done with these childish games. State what it is you wish of me and I'll do it. Is it a killing you desire or a fortress leveled?"

Jord's laughter was open and sincere. He was truly enjoying negotiating with this creature.

"It is not a killing I wish, though that may be necessary," said Jord, catching his breath. "It is your other gift that interests me most."

"Speak plainly, mortal," hissed the monstrous knight. "Surely a sickly Mabden, such as yourself, could have no need of service concerning love."

"Your insults keep you farther from your goal, fiend!" shouted Jord. "It would be better to send you back to the great dark god of the underworld and let him judge you and your attempted escape. How do you feel now about serving me, friend Raum, no matter what the task?"

It seemed that smoke steamed from the knight's flared nostrils. "Your point is well taken," he fumed.

"That is much better," smiled Jord. "Now I shall tell you what you must do. Among the Fins there is a king named Thorkuld. I hold no hatred for this king, but for his queen, Gudren, I have long held a great love."

"You wish the love of this woman?" asked Raum.

"Indeed I must possess her!"

"Your words tell me much," said Raum. "Possession is all that matters to you. Very well, I will bring her to you, but I shall not force her to love you for I doubt you would be able to return such feelings."

"Your insults matter not to me now, my loathsome friend. Just bring that sweet person to me." Sweat now dripped from the magician's feverish brow. He leaned forward as he spoke the strange words and erased the edge of the drawn circle of confinement.

King Thorkuld's great hall stood in the valley of Ever-spring. Here the grass remained green for the caribou and horses through all seasons, for this icebound stronghold was warmed by the steaming springs that fed the placid lake. Queen Gudren stood by the large windows overlooking the shining water as a handmaid braided her gold-white tresses. Her son, Prince Jal, now in his twelfth year, lay on a couch nearby studying a book of runes. The queen's cool, blue eyes gazed through the window toward the great fjord that marked the entrance into Ever-spring from the sea.

"When will Father return?" asked the boy absently.

"Soon," replied Queen Gudren.

"Why could I not go with him, Mother?" asked the Prince. "I am tall for my age and very good with a bow."

"The hunt is too dangerous. Your father explained this to you. Why must you act so childish? When you behave in this manner you are only telling the king that his son is not yet ready to become a man."

The prince threw his book aside and ran from the room. The handmaid hesitated, not sure of what she should do.

"Let him go, Gerda," said the queen. "He will see that his bad humor gains him nothing and he will grow a little closer to manhood." Her eyes clouded for a moment and then she said, "Some say I am too stern with my son. They say I should be more loving. But alas, I have little choice. I am the wife of the king and Jal is his son. When the time comes for . . . Jal to take the king's place he must have great strength and character. No one knows when that day will arrive, but it is my duty to the people to see that the new king is worthy."

"We do understand, Highness," said Gerda, her task of hairdressing completed.

"Gerda!" exclaimed the queen, pointing out the open window. "A sail! But not the king's!"

Gerda peered over the window ledge toward the river that joined the lake and fjord. Coming out of the shadows cast by the vaulted walls of granite and ice was a purple sail with red pennants flying. Above the sail hovered a cloud of dark birds whose cries could be heard across the lake.

"What is the emblem on that sail?" whispered the Queen.

"Too far, my lady," replied Gerda anxiously, "but wait! I can see it . . . oh no!"

"Then you read it as I do!" cried Gudren. "It is a black-winged death's-head. Who dares carry such a foul standard to Thorkuld's land?"

"May the gods spare us this omen!" moaned Gerda.

At that moment the booming sound of Ever-spring's signal horns was heard far away then answered loudly from the castle towers. Men-at-arms rushed from the gates and into the valley, a few were mounted on spirited horses.

"Oh, that the king were here!" cried the handmaid.

"Well, he is not here, Gerda," stormed the queen, turning on the servant girl in fury. "Stop your cowardly wailing and go find Prince Jal. I want him here with me and out of our warriors' way."

"Yes, Your Highness," cried Gerda dashing from the room.

The queen's slender fingers strayed to the jewel-studded blade in its sheath at her waist as she watched the boats move out into the lake.

The towering dark figure stood in the prow of the dragon-headed ship wrapped in his black, fur-trimmed cape. As the keel sliced the warm waters, Raum opened his shroudlike cloak to reveal he was armored and ready for battle. Behind him the oarsmen pulled hard, not content to let the full sail carry them to the lake's far shore. Between the oarsmen sat the blood-thirsty crew Raum had picked from among Jord's followers. He had not tested their ability to fight. He felt this was of little importance for he, himself, could probably carry out the mission alone. He did hope, however, that the appearance of his crew would so frighten the opposition that his task might be made simpler. The helmsman shouted to Raum, pointing, but the infernal knight had already seen the approaching boats. Near his hand, resting in its iron holder, was an oil-soaked fireband. He rubbed his hands over its charred surface and flame leaped forth instantly. The great, dark warrior then carried the torch back to where the men now crouched with bows and unlighted fire arrows. The ravens streamed across the shrinking distance between the war parties and shrieked their excitement to the eager combatants.

"Up oars!" bellowed Raum. The long oars were quickly shipped and now the oarsmen, too, prepared for battle.

In the approaching lead boat stood a tall red-faced man. He cupped his hand to his bearded mouth and shouted, "Stay you there and say your name or die now!"

Raum passed among the archers with the brand and lit the arrows. He then returned to his place near the dragonhead and exposed himself to full view of the onrushing Fins. The first boats seemed to slow a bit upon seeing the unholy figure in its black-winged helmet and glowing eyes. The sun glinted weakly on the giant's black breastplate.

"It is Raum you threaten," roared the awful voice. "It is Raum, Earl of the Netherworld and council to the Prince of Evil. Your turn has come to visit my world just as I visit yours!" His fiery eyes shifted to the archers. "Now!" he bellowed.

The missiles left a smoky path between the great death's-head ship and the native longboats. The iron-tipped arrows sank deep into the defending boats' hulls and soon had the Fin soldiers screaming and leaping into the water before they had launched a single arrow. The next volley cut down those few who had chosen to stay with their boats and fight the fire. Raum saw the red-bearded leader shout his curse before he dropped his upraised sword, his body sprouting a fine coat of feathered shafts.

"They swim to us, my lord," cried the helmsman.

"Throw the skins of oil over the sides," ordered Raum. His voice seemed almost touched with boredom. The oarsmen tossed the opened oilskins, then lowered the oars and pulled hard sending the great ship forward once more. The screams of the dying filled their wake as the oil-covered water sprang into a boiling inferno.

"There are more awaiting us on the shore, my lord," laughed the helmsman.

"Bowmen to the ready," commanded Raum.

A defending party had now assembled on the rocky shore barring the way to the high-walled castle. Their number appeared greater than Raum's invaders. The dark warrior cast aside his shield and all clothing save his helmet, breastplate and leather tunic. The helmsman decided his new captain was even more frightening now to the eye than when fully clothed. From one great hand dangled a large ax, from the other a broadsword of unbelievable length. Raum's silky black hair hung down his back in a single braid to facilitate his freedom of vision and movement.

"Release your arrows," called Raum.

Tiers of men collapsed on the shore under the deadly rain from Raum's archers, but then this rain was returned to the ship from the castle walls. Many of the invaders fell in pain tugging madly at the shafts protruding from various areas of their bodies. The ship slid through the breaking waves and ground ashore among the defenders, crushing many as it went. Raum's men were over the sides engaging the enemy before the ship settled lopsided with a groan of rock and wood. The air was immediately filled with the shouts of men and the clanging of weapons upon armor. Somewhere a horse cried out its terror and was joined by the din of ravens.

Above it all stood Raum, dark against the smoky sky. His gaze followed the castle wall until he spied the closed gate. With an evil smile he leaped from the ship's listing deck and cleaved a defender from shoulder to navel with his ax as his feet touched the blood-soaked shore. He was instantly set upon by three brave and determined Fins. He parried their blows and thrusts with the ax, then when they seemed about to attack in unison, Raum's long blade swung low and ended the battle for the three. He waded through death and carnage with the zest of a boy in a summer meadow. So certain and awful were this hellish warrior's weapons that soon a trail of dying and maimed soldiers extended from the ship to where Raum now stood before the gate. Five mounted men with long spears now charged him in defense of the gateway.

"Now you die, monster!" cried one of the riders

lowering his lance as his horse galloped down upon the crouched demon-knight.

Raum's laughter could be heard above the clamor of battle as he threw his great sword. The horse's front legs buckled as soon as the blade entered its broad chest, cleanly piercing the beast's heart.

Raum's ax severed the man's head before he had touched the earth, the falling mount having thrown him. The bloody giant swung the headless body into the path of two other charging horses. One fell, its feet tangled, and the other swerved wildly making the rider fall and release his lance. The big spear was in Raum's hand immediately and none too soon, for the two remaining gate defenders now rode down upon him and only by his uncanny awareness of all about him was Raum able to turn in time and swing the lance into their charge. One of the men flew over him as though he had wings and fell near his fellow who had been unhorsed moments before. Raum's ax broke the other's fall momentarily and he died watching the great flat blade draw tangles of entrails from the wound in his stomach.

Raum, now smeared with the gore of others, went to the dead horse and tugged his blade free. The three fallen and dazed guards saw the towering black figure above them for only a moment. This was the last thing they were to see in this life.

As Raum stood cleaning his weapons with the cloak of a fallen guard a sharp little spasm of pain shot through his thigh. He quickly plucked the arrow from his dusky flesh and stared upward at the small figure on the top of the stony wall. He was only a boy, bow in hand, yellow hair floating in the wind.

"You shall die a thousand deaths when the king returns!" shouted the boy.

"Your death, brave imp, shall not have to wait so long," laughed Raum. He turned to the gate and struck it several times with the broad ax. Wherever the blade struck, flames burst forth and soon the thick timbers crackled angrily with fire and smoke. Now the lad was joined on the wall by others who began sending arrows and other missiles Raum's way. He stood close to the wall suffering only a few nicks before his men came charging up from the beach. Bodies began falling about him from above as his archers found their marks. Raum stepped to the burning gate and with a single kick sent the timbers falling inward. The invaders ran into the courtyard before the great hall of Thorkuld shouting their thirst for blood and plunder. Defenders swarmed upon them from all quarters, but Raum paid them little mind, for the treasure he sought stood above him in a window, her white braids hanging over the sill. He smiled, large fangs showing, when he saw the metallic glint of the blade she held.

Two guards barred his way into the castle proper. Raum would have enjoyed toying with them were it not for his yearning to return to Iceland, to be freed of Jord's commission, and to begin his search for the one called Merlin. The guards realized too late he had only been playing with them. Their deaths were swift and clean.

Queen Gudren cringed against the wall clutching the ornate blade to her breast. Beyond the door to her chamber all was chaos and shouting. The grief she felt for her dying people was eclipsed only by her fear for Prince Jal's safety. Gerda had never returned with the boy and now the queen felt that death would come without her seeing her son or the king ever again.

The sounds of fighting beyond the queen's door suddenly ended and now only Gerda's screams could

be heard coming nearer, nearer. The locked door was
shattered by a huge ax and was kicked into the room
in a shower of splinters. The doorway was filled with
the most terrifying figure Gudren had ever seen. The
awesome knight dragged the screaming handmaid into
the room and threw her at her mistress' feet. Gudren's
eyes were wide with horror. She drew her arm back
holding the blade ready to strike.

"Why are you . . . why . . . what do you want?"
whispered the queen.

Raum's coarse features broke into a smile that made
his dark face even more terrifying. You would be
Queen Gudren?" he demanded.

She did not reply.

"Forgive my manners," smiled Raum bowing deeply.
"I am Raum in the service of Jord, Seer of Iceland,
who craves the company of Your Highness."

"Jord!" cried the queen. "I should have known he
would have a hand in this, the saddest day of my life.
My husband, the king, will never permit you to take
me to Jord. Nor would King Uln of Iceland allow it."

"King Uln has long been in the power of Jord. You
shall gain no help from him . . . nor from your husband, my lady."

"What do you mean?" she gasped.

"Thorkuld and his party lie dead beneath an avalanche of ice."

Gudren's eyes fluttered and grew dim; the knife
slipped from her fingers and clattered to the stone floor.
Slowly she slid to her knees. Gerda, sobbing, embraced
the queen and held her in her arms.

"All . . . all gone," moaned the queen.

Suddenly Raum's head jerked about, his blazing
eyes searching the doorway. He strode silently to a
position in the shadows near the door, his sword at

the ready. A man crept through the entryway and Raum's great hand closed on his neck.

"My lord!" choked the man as he was lifted from the floor. " 'Tis I, Harek, your helmsman!"

Raum dropped the man whose complexion had turned an ugly violet. "Why do you skulk about here?" asked Raum. "Is there no more fighting to be done elsewhere?"

"The castle has fallen, my lord," said Harek getting to his feet and rubbing his bruised neck. "We have enlisted the survivors to begin loading the spoils aboard ship."

"You have not answered me," growled Raum. "What brought you to these quarters?"

"I was looking for the lad I saw dash up the stairway yonder. He killed one of my best oarsmen with his bow."

Both the queen and Gerda became still at the mention of the boy.

"I wager he was a blond gangling lad in a blue tunic," grinned Raum.

"That he was," replied Harek.

"You have no woman, do you Harek?" asked the dark knight. "You may take that dark-haired one lying there if you like."

"Bless you," said the seaman with a broad smile.

"I am going after the boy," said Raum. "It is his wound, and his only, that I carry from today's sport. Stay and guard the women while I make him pay for his marksmanship."

"No!" screamed the queen.

"Just as I thought," laughed Raum. "The brat with the bow would be your son, my lady. That is good. I go to fetch him now and I shall not kill him so long as you do my bidding. That would include returning with us to Iceland and Jord. Do not consider taking

your own life now for it is you who keeps the boy
alive. If you die, I have no further use for a pesky
boy. I think you see my meaning, my lady."

The dazed queen nodded her head and Raum
slipped noiselessly from the room. He closed his eyes
once he had gained the hallway and concentrated. He
"felt" the boy's presence somewhere to the left and
above him. He found a small doorway leading to the
tower and moved slowly up the steps. The boy's back
was to him when the huge warrior slipped up behind
him. The young prince was staring down into the
horror that was once the courtyard of his home.

Jal jumped so badly at the sound of Raum's voice
that he nearly toppled from the high window. "Come
along, my princely whelp!" boomed Raum.

He roared with laughter at the boy's shock and
swatted his narrow buttocks with his sword. The youth's
eyes were wide with terror. His lips moved but no
sound came.

"Speak up, brat," laughed Raum.

"I said you are a coward and an animal!" shouted
the boy.

Raum's hand raised to strike but, remembering his
pledge and terms with the queen, he only reached out
and grabbed the boy about the waist and carried him,
kicking, from the room.

During the long days and nights at sea Prince Jal
stayed close to either his mother, the queen, or the
helmsman, Harek, whom Raum had caused him to feel
friendship toward by saying a few strange words over
the lad's head as he slept. Harek was quite receptive to
the boy's friendship and admired the spirit he showed
even to Raum.

Although Gerda now wore the collar of bondage to

Harek, the helmsman was content to permit her to stay at the queen's side. Once they were home he would demand her time and attention.

The queen spoke to none, other than Gerda and Jal. She spent her days staring at the back of the dark giant that either stood or sat in the bow at all times. She would awaken at night to find him standing silent in the moonlight. She wondered if he ever slept.

The ship's progress was slow since they had lost all but two oarsmen and the sail was now their sole source of power. The ship also sat very low in the water due to its load of booty. Only a handful of warriors survived to share this prize. These men had brought a few women captives with them, two of which now prepared and served the food to all aboard the ship.

And there were the ever-present ravens drifting overhead or perching on the mast or prow of the ship.

After endless days of seeing only the back of her dreadful captor, Queen Gudren was startled to find him gazing at her when she awoke one sunless morning. She held and returned his gaze for a few moments until Raum motioned her to come to him. She looked about her. Prince Jal, Gerda and the others slept. The queen pulled her cloak about her shoulders and quietly stood to face Raum. Again he signaled her to approach him. She moved forward careful not to disturb the sleepers.

When she was an arm's length from him she stopped and asked in a coldly quiet voice, "You would speak with me, my lord?"

Your voice is like your eyes, my lady," rumbled the knight. "They have the feel of chilled steel. I would indeed speak with you. I feel your eyes on me much of the time. I should like to know your reason for this.

Is it hatred, wonder at my power, or perhaps simply lust?"

"Silence!" spat the outraged queen. "You forget who you address, foul killer of the innocent!"

"I think 'tis you who forgets," laughed Raum. "You, fair lady, are nothing more than a prisoner and I your master . . . at least until I hand you over to your lover." He laughed mirthlessly.

"Have you no mercy?" she cried through clenched teeth.

"I fear that mercy is one emotion that I know nothing of."

"As evil as I know you are, I believe you speak the truth. You do not feel mercy or compassion! Who . . . what are you, really?"

"Is that why you stare at me so?" he asked, no longer smiling. "Very well, troubled lady, I shall answer your questions, but I must warn you my answers will only trouble you more. As to my true identity, I am Raum, Earl of Netherworld, Vassal of Lucifer. The magician, Jord, had summoned Lord Asteroth, my superior, in his conjurations but I persuaded Asteroth to let me come in his stead. I seek to escape the environs of the Underworld and find one among you mortals who may aid me. His name is Merlin and he dwells among the Britons in the southern isles."

She stepped back from him and gasped, "Then you are a demon! A demon who seeks the aid of a mortal? And why do you serve the loathsome creature Jord?"

"The Druid may possess information I have long sought, information not available in my realm. As for my service to Jord, it is a simple matter. I do this single task for his sake and he shall free me to enter the world and pursue my quest."

"Did you speak the truth when you told of my husband's death?"

"Yes, my lady."

"How do you come by this knowledge?"

"I know he and his party were killed in an avalanche for it was of my making. I possess a gift for such things."

"Ooooh," moaned the sad queen. "I thought I could hate you no more but you draw even more from me!" She lunged for the poniard in his belt sheath but his hand closed on her white arm and held her fast.

"Although I may cause feelings of love among you mortals, they are feelings I cannot experience. If I were to say I feel sorrow for you, my lady, you would know that I lie, for I can feel nothing for you other than a desire to possess your fair body.

"Unhand me, carrion!" she screamed. Prince Jal, like the other sleepers, was awakened by the queen's shrill voice. Upon seeing his mother struggling in the arms of his hated enemy, the boy leaped to his feet and snatched a sword from a nearby guard who was still numb with sleep.

"No, lad!" called Harek from his position at the helm.

Jal hesitated a moment glancing back at his new friend.

"He'll kill both you and the queen," cried Harek. "Drop your blade!"

Raum grinned broadly when he saw the enraged boy plunge the sword tip into the deck. His hands released their hold on the queen. Ugly bruises now marred her smooth flesh.

Queen Gudren ran to her son and led him back to their place aft. She held the boy close as they lay down. Gerda covered them with a heavy fur blanket.

Raum turned away and resumed his solitary watch of sea and sky.

A great pavilion had been erected in honor of Raum's victorious return with Queen Gudren. Jord, it appeared, was as taken with the booty as he was with the beautiful queen. Strong wine and fresh-roasted meats were served at the banquet table. Raum ate heartily as did his crew.

Jord had the queen chained to his dais at the head of the feast board, but even then the hate-filled woman neither spoke nor looked at the magician. This amused Raum and he chuckled as he ate. Not knowing what caused the dark knight's mirth, Jord leaned to inquire.

"Your spirits are high, Lord Raum," said Jord, "as well they should be, but tell us what causes your open laughter."

"Honesty," laughed Raum.

"A strange trait and an evasive answer for one of your origin," said Jord, irritated. "Tell me," he continued, viewing Jal beside Harek farther down the table, "how is it the young prince shows such esteem for your helmsman?"

"That would be my work, friend Jord," smiled Raum. "I felt it best if the boy had one among us he would trust and give heed to. He can be most bothersome."

"I can hardly believe a nose-drip child of twelve could annoy such as you," commented Jord.

"Do not underestimate Prince Jal," warned Raum. "His well-aimed arrow was the only wound I received among the Fins."

"I shall have him killed for you," laughed Jord.

"I much prefer to do my own killing," replied Raum. Jord's spirits were also high and he laughed at what he took to be the demon's cruel humor. He then turned his attention to Queen Gudren. "Why do you not eat?" he asked. "I should think you would be filled with hunger after your long voyage." He touched her hair but she jerked away from his greasy hand. "Perhaps a kiss would whet your appetite," laughed Jord.

"Your lips would only taste my vomit," hissed Gudren without looking at the startled magician.

"Such words are ill-suited to so lovely a lady," complained Jord. "Perhaps you lack a proper respect for me. You have never seen my power at work."

"Nothing you might do could make me feel you to be any more than the dung of sick dogs," she stated.

Raum roared his laughter. "Our lady can give pretty speeches when called upon," he said breathlessly.

"Perhaps," said Jord to the queen, his eyes bulging with rage, "you would prefer the company of some of my friends from the dark realms."

"I have had that pleasure," she replied coolly, "with your lackey, Raum."

"Ah! So he has told you of his origin. Well, my lady, I would not want you to think all from that region are as handsome as our gallant Raum. There are many who do not resemble men at all."

"Such as yourself, fool?" she laughed bitterly.

"Your insults grow tiresome, cold woman."

"Then I should think you would no longer desire my company."

Jord suddenly seized her throat, shaking and screaming his wrath. "It is your tongue I would put away, madam! One word and I shall cut it from your mouth!"

"As you please," answered Gudren hoarsely. "All I have to say to you will always be in my eyes. Shall you blind me also? Tell me then, Jord, what kind of bride shall you have in me?" Her laughter bubbled forth from her constricted throat.

He flung her to the floor and raised a hand to strike her. Now, all had been listening and watching this exchange as though it were the evening's entertainment, especially Raum; but now a cry rang out from the far end of the table and a slight figure charged up its length through food and drink.

"Jal!" shouted Harek, but too late. With the helmsman's own stolen knife the young prince flung himself upon Jord, sinking the blade deep into the magician's chest.

Raum wrenched the blade from Jal's grasp and held him helpless against the table. Gudren stared up at this dark tormentor and at Jord as he swayed above her peering down at the crimson life flowing from his breast. He raised his eyes to Raum as if to say something but was met only with the demon knight's sardonic smile before falling to the floor dragging food and wine with him. All was silent as the magician breathed his last beneath the table, then shouted threats and curses filled the air.

Harek was immediately beside Raum and the prince with drawn sword. "Stand back," he warned to those who would avenge Jord.

"You be the fool, Harek," growled an old hornhelmet. "The boy is not your son!"

"Nor is he mine," bellowed Raum stopping the advancing men with the force of his voice, "but I will tell you this, no one touches the boy without suffering at my hands!"

"Why do you take this stand?" It was the queen who spoke as she now stood shaken beside the table.

"Do not question good fortune, my lady," hissed Harek.

"The lad has done me a great service," said Raum with an oily smile. "It makes no difference that it was not his intention. I was in bondage to Jord and it was him only who could release me into the world to undertake my quest."

"But how so have I helped you?" asked the boy weakly.

"Only Jord's word or death could free me. The law dictates that I am powerless against he who had made the magic circle. You, Prince Jal, were under no such law."

"Then I have freed you whom I have longed only to kill!" cried Jal in open despair.

"I know," laughed Raum, enjoying the irony.

"Release your hold on my son," demanded the queen. "You are not fit to touch the lowest of men, to say nothing of a prince. Go back to your doomed land for you cannot hope to ever be worthy of life among men."

"My lady," said Raum, his fangs showing as he spoke, "do not make me regret the discovery of this new sensation I now feel. I believe you Mabden would call it gratitude. Ah, but it was only fleeting," he concluded, raising his sword to the boy's throat.

"My lord," pleaded Harek, "I have come to feel like a father to the spirited lad. Return both Queen Gudren and her son to their homeland and I shall serve you in whatever way you choose."

Raum pondered the seaman's bargain for a few moments then released the boy to his mother's arms. Those gathered about the four cringed before Raum's alien gaze as it swept their ranks. "Remember," he roared, "I shall give any who harm the boy or queen a slow death . . . a very slow death." He turned to Harek and said, "Get your crew assembled. I think another night in Iceland would not be healthy for any of us."

"By the gods!" swore Harek.

"What now, helmsman?" demanded Raum.

"There will be none here that we might trust for crew."

Raum turned his fiery eyes upon the gathered warriors once more and shouted, "I want supplies aboard my ship now! If the ship is not made ready by nightfall I shall begin killing and you must believe me, I shall kill you all and enjoy it."

The western sky was the color of the great death's-head sail when it caught the evening wind and pushed the vessel toward the open water. Harek alone maneuvered the ship, there was no other crew. The queen and Jal sat among the provisions amidships. Raum had taken his place in the bow near the evil figurehead. The wind remained with them until all light had fled from the sky and left only bright stars above.

"I fear we've entered a calm, my lord," called Harek. It was then that he noticed a movement among a large bundle of furs. From her hiding place crawled Gerda. He laughed as she darted to the queen's side.

Raum returned the laugh and said to Harek, " 'Twould seem you'll never be rid of that one."

"Nor do I wish to be," confessed Harek. He continued to check the dying breeze. "I wager we shall drift off course this night without wind or oarsmen," he said.

Raum was silent for a moment, his eyes glowing hotly in the darkness, and then he said, "Queen Gudren, would you be so good as to take Prince Jal and your maid astern and remain there with Harek for the remainder of the voyage?"

"For what purpose?" she asked sharply.

"We are about to take on our new crew and I am sure they will not be the sort with whom you would care to mingle."

"I do not understand . . ." she began to protest.

"Silence! Do as you are told for once, good lady, and earn the service I offer."

"What service?" raged the queen.

"I deliver you into life, my lady, 'though my better mind tells me your death would be more satisfying. My resolve weakens each time you resist my orders."

"Come, Mother," said Prince Jal, "I'm sure he means what he says, he is only an animal . . . or worse."

"A pity the lad has your tongue, my lady," said Raum sullenly.

"When my tongue was used against Jord you found it amusing, Lord Raum," smirked the queen.

Raum walked toward them weighing a slender and very sharp poniard in his hand. "I shall take a finger from the lad for each moment you tarry, my willful queen."

Gerda cried out and pulled her mistress to her feet. Jal followed the ladies along the deck to where Harek sighed his relief.

Raum knelt to the smooth planking of the ship's deck and with the tip of the slender blade cut a strange design, murmuring words in an unknown tongue. This completed, he returned to the bow and raised his arms skyward, chanting. The ravens could be heard coming across the darkened waters first. Then a second sound was heard by those on board but understood by none save Raum. The sea seemed to groan against the ship's hull, a green glow shining from its surface now.

"What is it, Harek?" asked Jal.

"I couldn't say, lad," replied the man, "but I think we best stay right here as Lord Raum ordered."

Gerda was the first to see them. She began screaming and Harek held her close, placing his hand over her mouth. Slowly they came, pulling their decayed and weed-laced bodies over the side from the sea. They were the damned of the sea come to do their lord's bidding. The green nimbus surrounded them and the ravens swept to and fro in the eerie light. Each of the shambling horrors took a place at the locks and hoisted the long oars. At Raum's command the heavy paddles dropped beneath the waves and they were underway once more.

Many hours later when a storm overtook them the ghastly crew lowered the sail and pulled resolutely at the oars. Queen Gudren, Jal, Harek and Gerda huddled beneath a blanket of sealskin in the stern. Standing above them at the helm was Raum shouting his commands to the hellish crew over the crash of thunder and sea. It seemed to go on for hours, but eventually the waves calmed and the first light of morning could be seen through the ragged clouds. The ravens had been perched and clinging to the ship during the tempest and now took flight across the water. Raum guided the craft after them.

"I fear we've been blown from our course, my lord," said Harek, coming out from under his cover.

"The ravens sense the direction of land," replied Raum. He relinquished the helm to Harek, saying, "Just follow them."

"Aye, but to what land?" asked Harek with concern.

"It will be the coast we seek," smiled Raum. "The queen and her son shall be home soon."

"And what then, my lord?"

"Then you shall fulfill your pledge to me, friend Harek."

"How so, my lord?"

"You shall be my helmsman and take me to the isles of the Britons."

"Shall this then be our crew, sir?" asked Harek with revulsion.

"They are dependable, but if you find others more to your liking then pray enlist them. We have gold enough to pay them well."

"I take it, my lord," spoke Queen Gudren, who was joining them with Jal and Gerda close behind, "that you do not intend to tarry in our kingdom."

"Indeed not, my lady," he replied.

"A wise decision," said Prince Jal, "for soon I would devise some way to slay you, my lord."

"Jal!" snapped the queen.

"The prince is truthful," laughed Raum. "He does not let the fact that I have spared, yea even saved, your lives confuse him. Vengeance is what he most desires."

"One day, sir," said the youth, "I shall have my vengeance. It will be my hand that stills your dark heart."

The queen was frightened to see Raum no longer smiling but gazing levelly at the impassioned prince. "I still do not understand," she said quickly, "what it is you wish to learn from the one called Merlin."

"I fear you could not understand," said Raum.

"Do not condemn me for a simpleton without first testing me," she smiled.

"Very well," he sighed. "Long before your Mabden histories began, even before the gods had entered the world, there was a rebellion in the highest realms. Those in rebellion were cast out, after a time, and confined to the nether regions. The Highest was victorious and deemed it just that those who had challenged the Law of One should be thus confined. I was one of those so condemned."

"Perhaps, Lord Raum," said the queen frowning, "you were right in your judgment of my powers to comprehend. 'Tis difficult to follow such ideas when there is nothing akin in our tribal teachings. I am also at a loss to understand what connection this Merlin has with such things."

"His knowledge of these lost histories and the workings of certain principles are great in value to me."

The queen looked deep into those hot, yet somber, eyes for a moment. She then placed a hand on the knight's heavy arm. "I believe I know your quest, my lord," she said softly. "You seek to return to your first state and home. I feel pity for you . . . the murderer of my beloved husband, for I should consider your chances of achieving that which is most desired by you to be completely impossible."

"Your pity is not asked for, received, nor understood," said Raum testily.

"You feel the old Briton holds clues to your quest?" she asked, ignoring his show of temper.

"Perhaps."

"I promise you," said Prince Jal suddenly, "I shall not trouble you with feelings of pity, my lord. I shall devote my time to praying that the Britons spare your life until such time as I might come and claim it."

"Enough, Prince Jal!" ordered Harek.

"Mind how you speak to me, devil's lackey," retorted the boy.

Harek's face winced with the pain of the lad's words. "All that I have done has been for my young lord's sake and the queen's. It is for you that I now suffer bondage to Lord Raum."

"Do not claim nobility for acts that are merely a common decency," said Jal angrily.

Gerda started to protest against the prince's attitude and to defend the man who was her captor, but the queen's hand raised in an unspoken command to silence.

"Ahead, my lady," said the hulking knight quietly. "The cliffs of the great fjord."

"Home!" cried Gudren. "Quickly, Lord Raum, dismiss your awful crew that my people might know that I am returned free and in no danger."

"Ah," laughed Raum, "and upon seeing this hated ship, manned only by a crew of two, your people are sure to set upon us, before explanations could be given. The crew shall stay, my lady, but not set foot ashore."

They were now entering the fjord, its walls of stone and ice dwarfing the ship. Before they emerged from the shadow of the great cliffs into Ever-spring the sentry horns were sounding. Raum could see a great many boats coming toward them from across the lake. He turned to the queen and said, "Perhaps it would be wise for you to stand in the bow, my lady, that you may be seen before the crew or myself."

"I should let them come and destroy you, but I am still able to show some gratitude for my return," she said as she left them and cautiously made her way past the horrid crew. She refused to let her eyes look fully upon these condemned souls and drew her cloak about her, although the air was now quite warm.

The others stood about Harek as he brought the ship through the river mouth and into the lake to face the nearing fleet. Prince Jal smiled crookedly, his long blond hair shadowing his eyes. "Would it be your in-

tention to remain aboard with the crew, my lord?" he
asked of Raum.

"That would be my intention, for I am anxious to be
on my way," replied the demon-knight.

"And we are anxious that you be on your way," said
the boy coldly.

Harek bit his lip as he watched the two from the
corner of his eye. He knew Raum would take little
more from the arrogant lad. Gerda stood back, frightened but silent. Harek noted, with sadness, that the
handmaid was still little more than a child, herself,
and still very innocent. He resolved that her innocence
remain intact until such time as he would return from
the southern isles. "Gerda!" he called and motioned
the startled girl to his side.

Raum watched, openly puzzled, as she went to the
helmsman and stood trembling beside him. Harek
gently removed Gerda's collar of bondage and cast it
into the lake. He then kissed her, but the frightened
girl shrank from him for she, too, could not understand
the man's actions.

At Harek's command the sail was lowered and the
oarsmen moved the ship at a leisurely pace to meet
the arriving boats. The queen now cast off her cloak
and stood in the wind, her hair and gown billowing
about her. A great shout went up from the lead boat
as the queen was recognized. Then cries of dismay and
horror were heard when the crew of Raum's ship
came into view.

"Hold!" shouted Gudren. "This ship comes in peace.
Lay aside your weapons and bring a boat alongside
that I and my son might be in your company as we
return home."

As this was done Harek breathed a sigh of relief,
for there were far more war boats than when first he

came to this placid lake. They must have come from all parts of Thorkuld's kingdom following his death and the abduction of the queen and prince. He now realized that these people had begun to prepare for war with Iceland. He shuddered as he thought of how his actions had contributed to what might have meant the destruction of much of his homeland and people.

The ship now lay becalmed in the water, as the long-boats of armed warriors circled warily. One moved in to take Gudren and Jal from the ship's deck. Raum stood beside the mast, never speaking, as the two women and Jal stepped to the smaller craft. None cast a backward glance. The dark giant smiled ruefully at his helmsman's sadness.

When the boat had cleared the ship Raum roared his command, "Up sail!" Several of the gruesome crew pulled at the lines hoisting the deep-violet cloth high. Raum looked sharply about the ship, then to Harek who worked frantically steering the vessel away from the boats as the wind suddenly caught and filled the death's-head sail.

"My lord!" cried Harek, "why do we hurry in such a reckless manner?"

At that moment Jal shouted something from the queen's boat to those who circled nearby. In one of these stood a tall man in burnished breastplate. He put a horn to his lips and sent a loud call across the water. His trump was echoed by another far down the lake near the river's mouth, through which they had just sailed to enter Ever-spring.

"Does that answer your questions, friend Harek?" shouted Raum, taking his place beside the seaman, blade drawn. "Our young prince has lied to us. He does not want us to leave as soon as he said. I am afraid we have much blood to spill before this day is through."

"We move at a goodly pace now, my lord," said Harek anxiously. "If we might gain the open sea none could catch us!"

"Ah, but look," laughed Raum, suddenly seeming to be in high spirits. "Something is amiss at the river. A barricade!"

"They have stretched a net of rope across the river's entrance," shouted Harek. "We will ram this flimsy barrier and be on our way before any can draw a blade."

"Your good news is ill founded, my friend," smiled Raum. "Look beneath the trees at either side of the net. Boats! They intend to stop us, that is plain enough."

Raum glanced behind them to discover the mass of war boats now in earnest pursuit. Prince Jal, having left the queen's boat for one filled only with fighting men, now stood in the bow of the lead boat waving a sword.

"Your young friend is determined to be in on the kill," said Raum to Harek. When the helmsman saw the pursuing boy his face paled visibly.

"How is it he changed so once we neared his home?" asked Harek sadly. "I am sure he felt kindly toward me in the beginning."

"Indeed he did," said Raum, "for I, myself, cast the spell that made it so. I felt he would be much easier to manage if he were to respect you and your words."

"But why has the spell left?"

"To undo a variety of magical spells, one must reverse one's movements back to where the spell was first manifest. When the ship arrived at the place where

Prince Jal first experienced the enchantment its effect and the power were ended."

"I do miss the lad," said Harek, "with his friendly face. The lady Gerda I miss, also."

"Lay such human feelings aside, Harek, for yonder comes the enemy!"

"And what weapons our sorry crew have are either broken or rusted," complained the seaman.

The grim oarsmen leaned hard to their task and the sail was taut with wind. "Smoke, my lord!" cried Harek, pointing.

A blue veil of smoke drifted out from where the native boats rested under the overhanging trees. "Ah ha!" spat Raum, his red eyes narrowing, "they mean to give us a taste of what we offered when first we met them."

"They mean to burn us?" asked Harek cooly.

"Aye, that would be their hope. We must hit the net with force enough to pass through or they will surely burn us to the water."

"But look!" shouted Harek foresaking his previous calm. "They will not hold their fire so long!"

Great flaming javelins arched majestically from the forest at water's edge. Harek worked hard to change the fast-moving vessel's course, but to no avail. As three of the long spears pierced the sail its cloth ignited. Other of the missiles struck the ship proper and Raum was hard pressed to extinguish the resulting fires. The grisly oarsmen continued their work as if in a dream.

"Steady yourself, my lord," called Harek, "we are upon the net!"

The ship pitched and groaned as the great tangle of rope seized it and checked its rush toward the fjord and passage to the sea. Much of the ship was now engulfed in flames. The oarsmen sat their stations trying to force the prow through the clinging web.

"Lord Raum!" warned Harek, "the bow is breaking up!"

"Quickly," shouted Raum, "into the net! The ship is lost!"

Clouds of sparks and fire flared about their feet as they raced down the deck and leaped into the smoke, hoping their outstretched hands would find and hold the ropes. Raum's weight carried him beneath the water even though he clung to the net. He gazed upward to see Harek clamoring up the ropes and out of the water. Raum watched as the underside of the ship began to open with hissing bubbles of smoke and steam, spilling the crew into the churning brine. Raum made a sign to them with his armored fist and they vanished in a frothy swirl. The dark warrior then climbed upward through the sagging lines.

When the knight's head broke surface all was chaos about him. Flaming wreckage was tangled in the heavy net. Ravens swooped through the smoke screaming their excitement. On the net, not far from Raum's position, clung Harek with sword in hand. Advancing along the twisting barrier came the boats from shore. Many armed men stepped from the boats to the net to end any hope the two may have had of escape to the shore.

"Over the top, Harek!" ordered Raum. "The tide is going out and will carry us swiftly to the sea."

"Aye, that it will if we be able to swim," laughed Harek, scrambling up the knotted lines. Then there sounded a strange popping noise and several of the ropes parted, having been burned through.

"Take care!" called Raum, but too late. Harek had nearly gained the uppermost ropes when they began breaking. He lost his footing and fell backward, his legs twisted in the heavy strands.

"Hang on," urged Raum, "and my blade shall have you free in no time."

"Behind you!" cried Harek.

Raum swung instinctively and his great sword sliced through an arm of the man moving close behind him on the swaying web. The man fell screaming into the smoke and water below. He was replaced on the net by two others diverting Raum's attention from Harek's plight momentarily. He parried the men's thrusts until his opening came and soon the two hung tangled and lifeless among the ropes.

When Raum's eyes returned to the trapped helmsman he found Harek cutting savagely at his bonds. The knight was about to leap to aid the snared man when he heard a high boyish shout behind them.

"Now!" cried the youthful voice.

Arrows pelted Raum's armor, one entering his arm, but his attention was not upon his own pain, for he saw Harek stiffen, feathered shafts quivering from his back. The seaman's tortured eyes moved first to Raum and then to the oncoming boats. These eyes welled with tears, yet not from the pain of arrows. He was still staring at the boy who stood in the boat with upraised sword when the net gave way and plunged them into the boiling waves below.

The moon was high when the shadowy nude figure finished its task of burial in the dark forest. He sat near the fresh mound of earth cleaning his digging tools, a broadsword and ax. He could see the small fire he had made near the shore although he was sitting some distance away. He could also see his armor and clothing hanging near the blaze drying. Several ravens

alighted upon the mound and Raum made no move
to drive them away. The demon-knight was deep in
thought . . . troubled thought.

Raum, Earl of the Infernal Regions, subject of the
Prince of Evil, and now renegade of the Netherworld
was experiencing a feeling quite new to him. He
stared at the mound and remembered the helmsman
who had served him and whom he had addressed as
friend. When others had regarded the unearthly knight
with revulsion, Harek remained a loyal companion.
The warrior's great hands closed into tight fists. He did
not like this new feeling. It was pain yet unlike any
Raum had experienced to date. He wondered how long
such pain would last. The more he considered his
discomfort the angrier he became. At last he leaped to
his feet, intent on an incantation to summon the dead,
when he stopped short. A strange realization came to
him. It would do no good to call forth Harek's spirit.
It would not be good . . . good . . . Good! Never
had he thought in such terms before! When had he
become concerned as to the goodness of things?

He became aware of a familiar odor. He looked
up to find his campfire was now a virtual pillar of
flame. He lifted his sword and ax and strode to the
gyrating fire. The sulphurous, unwholesome odor now
filled the night air. "Who is it who comes unbidden?"
demanded Raum.

"Ah, 'tis only I, Asteroth, your superior and super-
visor," came a voice from the serpentine flame.

"Why do you come? Is it punishment you bring
from the Lord of Evil?"

A shrill peal of laughter rang out from the fire. "No,
no, Lord Raum. He has hardly missed you. After all,
you are not a personage of great prominence in Lucifer's realm."

"I have no stomach for your games, my lord," growled Raum. "State your business with me and be done with it."

"I have brought you a gift, that is all, my boy."

"What gift?"

"Look there," said Asteroth, "tethered among the trees."

A great, dark shape moved in the darkness of the forest. Suddenly Raum gave a shout of surprise. "My mount!"

"Indeed," said Asteroth, "for what is a knight without a proper horse?"

"That be true enough," agreed Raum, "and few horses I have seen among the Mabden could carry my weight well." He went to the trees and led the overwhelmingly powerful steed into the circle of fire-light.

Its back was higher than a man's head and his muscles flexed with unholy strength. His coat was the glossy black of a raven's wing. The beast's eyes shone bright and fiery as it stamped its great hooves upon the earth.

"But why do you trouble yourself with gifts for one who has deserted your ranks?" asked Raum cautiously.

"Because you amuse me, Lord Raum," came the reply. "I have watched you change into something unlike any from the lower realms. You have had this growing agitation and yearning for I know not what . . ."

"True," said Raum.

"Nor do you know, I wager, what it is you long for and seek among these mortals who can only despise you."

"That one which I have just buried did not despise me!"

"So, even the Mabden fool you. Make no mistake, Lord Raum, you will find none here who will keep your company willingly . . . oh, perhaps there is one thing of which I should warn you."

"At last we reach the truth," muttered Raum.

"Yes, my misguided knight, so we have. As your friend and advisor it has fallen to me to inform you that these feelings you have newly experienced have been costly for you. It is my sad duty," chuckled Asteroth, "to tell you that already you have lost your claim to immortality."

"What do you say?" demanded Raum.

"It is quite simple. From this day forward you shall have the ability to die just as men do. Did you not realize before that you could not be killed?"

"Of course," replied Raum, "but what happens if I die?"

"You shall then return to us for a time for our pleasure and sport. Naturally you will not retain your previous standing and authority. You will be like any other mortal."

"Do not be certain, my lord," said Raum, eyes flaring in anger. "There may be a time when I shall escape our evil lord and even death itself!"

Shrill laughter pierced the night air once again. "Oh, you are amusing, Lord Raum. Do not let me detain you any longer from riding off to your ridiculous and laughable fate."

"We shall see, my lord," stormed Raum.

The fire flared once and then, as the laughter faded, died to glowing coals. Raum cursed, kicking the embers about with his bare foot. He dressed himself and led his horse to the shore where the fjord opened to the sea.

"Yes," he mused to himself, "I was quite aware of

not being subject to death while walking the bottom of this fjord and river carrying the body of . . . of my friend. A friend killed by one he felt true kindness toward." His dark face contorted in evil resolution.

"You think me dead, Prince Jal?" he shouted. "Is that why none of your boats have come? Well, they shall never again come through your great fjord!"

He stretched forth a hand and muscles strained within his armor as the awesome power of his will was unleashed. The lofty crags trembled for a moment before crashing downward in a thunderous quake closing the passage to Ever-spring.

Raum mounted the great, black charger and rode through the moonlight southward, a cloud of ravens gliding in his wake.

PART 2

Among the Vikings

A THICK, CHILLING FOG hung over the marshes. As is always the case, a deep silence came with the fog. Therefore when a flock of frightened ducks flew from hiding among the reeds, old Teg, the boatman, was startled and a bit uneasy. His nerves had not been well of late due to the stories that travelers brought from the north. It was said something evil had entered the land of the Viking kings, something that left death and horror in its wake. It was an evil that escaped identity since the kings were at peace among themselves and no invading armies had been discovered.

"The bodies of fine young warriors are found most every day," cried one harried wayfarer. "In the wood and along the shore they find them, lips parted, but pale and silent to the witness of the awful deed. Camps and villages have been discovered where all was burned, including the poor souls who dwelt there."

Teg shuddered and pulled the wolf's-hide robe about his scrawny shoulders. He poked a stick into the fire that burned before his makeshift shelter of reeds and driftwood. From the shelter, the front of which was

53

quite open, he could see his large flatboat tied to the stunted trees. This is not to say Teg could actually see the boat, but only its dark shape against the light on the water. His sight was nearly gone and dim shapes of light and dark were all he now perceived. He spent these days of his latter years on the quiet waters of the inlets he knew so well, ferrying goods and people for what they were willing to pay him. Teg spent much of his lonely time remembering those days of youth and adventure when he had sailed the high seas among the Viking crews.

The grizzled boatman's head suddenly jerked to one side listening. "Strange," he whispered to himself, " 'tis ravens I hear. A rare thing to this region." His rheumy eyes stared into the cold light. Dark shadows wheeled before him and by their calls he knew them to be the ravens.

"Great Odin!" cried the old seaman. "Have you come for me?"

A twig snapped nearby. Teg's right hand tightened on the cudgel at his side. No sooner had he touched the club, than the light before him became obscured by a looming blackness.

"Who is it?" croaked the boatman.

"I seek the one who sails the barge," boomed a terrifying voice.

"The boat would be mine, sir," replied Teg, shaken by the power of the voice.

"I would have you take me and my animal across these waters to the land of the Danes."

"But, kind sir," cried Teg, "my vessel is not worthy of the open sea. I travel only in these marshlands and to ports along these shores."

" 'Tis the sea I must cross, old one."

"I know of no ships crossing to Danish ports," said

Teg trying to sooth the angry voice, "but if you were of a mind to be sailing to more southern ports . . ."

"What? You know of ships sailing southward?"

"As I am sure you know, sir, merchant vessels are few in these waters. 'Tis of the Viking fleet I speak. I do know mighty Wulfgar will soon put to sea for raids upon the Britons."

"You know this Wulfgar?"

Teg relaxed to a degree and said, "To be sure. I sailed with him until my poor eyes grew dim. I could ask him to sell you passage."

"And what might his price be?"

"Gold if you have it, sir."

"If I had gold your captain would only take it before cutting my throat. I am familiar with your Viking ways. What other price would he accept?"

"Ha!" cackled Teg warming to the exchange, " 'Tis true you are not entirely ignorant of our ways. Very well, the other price would be your sword and strength in service once you've reached those green isles."

"Take me to this man!" ordered the dark figure.

"And who shall I say wishes to speak to mighty Wulfgar?"

"Inform him that Raum, Earl of the Netherworld, has come to do him service."

Teg fell backward clutching his stick. "Odin protect us!" he prayed.

Wulfgar's great lodge stood high on the ground overlooking the bay. A finely carved dragon rested at the peak of the loft. Hatches in the sloping roof emitted columns of blue smoke. Before the entrance, on high poles, hung the standards of many a Viking noble.

Below, in the village, swarmed men, women and some children making ready the fleet of dragon-head ships floating in the bay. The fog was lifting and sunlight now streamed through the lofty pine branches.

Out in the bay lay a bar covered with rushes. From behind this cover came Teg's flatboat, its sail catching the morning rays. Teg sat hunched in the stern at the tiller. Forward in the vessel stood an imposing figure wrapped in black beside a dark steed of magnificent size. As the craft neared the rough-hewn dock, the villagers pressed forward to gaze upon a singularly fascinating face. It was dark in color, much like some of the prisoners from the lands to the far south, and seemed filled with sharp angles. It was the eyes however that most held their interest. Fiery red they were and yet chilling to any they looked upon. Looking from beneath a heavy, brooding brow, these eyes told the villagers they were in the presence of no ordinary man.

Upon the mammoth horse hung armor and the articles of knighthood. The stranger urged the animal from the boat and the timbers of the landing groaned their protest. The crowd quickly parted for their passage. Old Teg led the way through the village to the huge wooden hall.

"Who is this ugly stranger you bring us, Teg?" called someone in the crowd.

"Watch your tongue," warned the old man, "for if you knew his true nature, your heart would cease its beating from fright."

Although Teg was quite familiar with these surroundings, he used his cudgel to tap and feel his way along until they stood before the hall entrance.

"Best you wait here," said Teg to the big knight, "while I inform Wulfgar of your arrival. He is not one who enjoys such surprises."

Saying nothing, Raum turned his back to the crowd and began adjusting the harness of his mount. When his hand came into contact with the broadsword hanging in its scabbard from the saddle, a voice called out behind him, "You will leave the blade, for no stranger may enter Wulfgar's lodge armed."

Raum turned smiling, not taking his hand from the weapon. The man who faced him was a heavy-bearded warrior. Raum guessed him to be a guard. "Your Norse ways are well known to me," smiled Raum crookedly. "Only a fool would come into your midst unarmed."

The guard bristled and pulled an ax from a loop on his wide girdle. "Remove your hand from the blade or I shall remove the hand from your person," he threatened.

No eye was quick enough to catch Raum's lightning movement, for suddenly the great sword was bare and in the dark knight's hand. Quickly the startled guard raised his war ax only to see the strange intruder lunge and to feel a stinging in his arm. He staggered back in shock, as they all did, at the sight of the ax on the ground where it fell, a bloody hand still clutching it. The guard murmured something and went to his knees holding his suddenly shortened arm close to his body.

Raum stepped around the fallen man and entered the lodge, sword in hand. Women busied themselves about a large cooking fire near the center of the hall. Along its walls lounged the men and women of Wulfgar's elite. Raum noticed that most of the men were heavily armed. They ceased their talking, aware of Raum's presence, as he moved past the fire to where Wulfgar sat on a crude throne.

The Viking chieftain was thick through his middle, but heavy muscles were still in evidence in his shoulders and limbs. His gray hair was long and unkept, while his beard hung in two neat braids. His nose

was red and bore an ugly scar. Bright blue eyes
sparkled from beneath shaggy brows. Old Teg sat
cowering at the leader's feet.

The boatman, noticing the hush settling upon the
gathering, asked anxiously, "Has he come, my lord?"

"He has," replied Wulfgar with a resounding belch.
A table heavy with food and drink was at his side.
"Come forward, your lordship," laughed Wulfgar, "and
welcome to our lodge."

Raum stepped before the aging chieftain, noting the
sound of steel being drawn about the smoky room.
"Has the blind one told you of my need to reach that
land ruled by Arthur?"

"Teg has told me . . . ah . . . I have already forgotten your name," smiled Wulfgar.

"My name is Raum and may not be soon forgotten if
your men do not step back and sheathe their blades."

"He has already severed Jutta's hand!" came a shout
from the back of the hall.

Wulfgar's smile remained fixed upon his shaggy face.
"If I were to grant you passage with us, you have gold
to give, of course."

"None," lied the demonic knight. "I have only my
service to offer in your defense."

"If you are who you have told Teg you are, how am
I to trust your word?" countered Wulfgar.

"And I could ask the same," shot back Raum. "We
at least start with equal reputations."

Wulfgar roared his laughter, then said, "The people
we face are not to be taken lightly, Lord Raum. It
may be true you are a very large man, but how well
do you perform in battle? How shall I know you to be
who you say you are?"

"Will your bantering never cease?" spat Raum. He
pointed a metaled finger to the cooking fire and it

flared as he spoke in an unknown tongue. Sparks flew about the beams overhead and the women ran screaming from the hall.

Raum turned back to Wulfgar only to find himself facing two warriors with drawn swords.

"We mean to test your strength, loud talker," hissed one as they advanced.

"Will your magic tricks aid you in facing cold steel?" asked the other.

"None shall be needed for the likes of you," laughed Raum going into a crouch, blade before him. "If you need your fighting men, Wulfgar," he said, "you had best restrain these two or the cooking fire shall be their funeral pyre."

"Coward!" shouted one of the men leaping forward and swinging his blade high. Sparks flew as Raum parried the blow. The knight's free hand crashed down in a mailed fist to the back of the man's neck. The sound of breaking bone brought shouts of delight from Wulfgar.

The other man was fast upon Raum jabbing at his unprotected middle. The unearthly warrior spun aside bringing the pommel of his sword crashing into the man's face. He went down screaming in pain and blindness. Raum's blade deftly slit the tormented man's throat.

"A craftsman!" shouted Wulfgar clappping his thick hands.

Raum pitched the bodies into the fire and strode to the table beside Wulfgar where he gulped the contents of a large cup. He then belched loudly into the Viking chief's face and said, "Do I sail with you or not? Give your answer now!"

"You sail, my lord," sighed Wulfgar openly pleased

with his guest. "You shall sail on my ship and give me good company."

The heavy odor of burning human flesh filled the smoky interior and most of those gathered fled the hall for fresher air.

"The stench seems to bother you naught, friend Raum," laughed Wulfgar.

"It is an odor one can become accustomed to," said Raum, "until it seems a fragrance."

"You amuse me greatly," laughed Wulfgar wiping his eyes. "You must tell me of your homeland."

"I'll not be your minstrel or jester. Besides, it would seem you will know these things soon enough."

Wulfgar's smile vanished. "Do you read my future or is your intent to threaten me?"

"Neither," laughed Raum. "No matter when one comes to my land it is always too soon."

"Ah, to be sure," roared Wulfgar relaxing once more. "Have more wine, my friend."

"To a bountiful journey," toasted Raum.

"Tell me now, my lord," urged the Viking, "was it not you who caused the dire stories coming from the north?"

"I have been north, 'tis true," said Raum picking up a piece of roasted meat. "I have also been given to killing those who would challenge me or bar my way."

"I shall pay Teg well for this day's work," said Wulfgar in admiration. "Where has that old one gone?"

"He left with the others," said Raum, his bared fangs tearing at the juicy meat.

Strong winds caught the Viking fleet's sails and soon the inlets were left far behind. Once in open water the oars were shipped and the vessels of war raced before the wind in a southwesterly course.

Raum stood beside Wulfgar marveling at the beauty of the gaudy sails, the swelling green sea and the high spirits of the crew. As they worked, these battle-scarred men chanted and shouted in chorus of love, life, war and the sea. The alien knight noted that if these men were as adept at fighting as they were at seamanship there was little wonder that the southern coastal villages lived in terror of them.

"What thoughts are in that evil head of yours?" asked Wulfgar, nudging Raum's ribs with his elbow. "You look almost mortal."

Raum paid little mind to the Viking's good-natured insults. "I was wondering at your people's obvious love of the sea."

"Ah, could it be any different?" sighed Wulfgar. "The sea is like our mother. All that we have comes from her. So little of our land is fit for tilling. The winters are too harsh in most areas for even a crop of wheat. Thus we must fish the sea and sail to those places that have the things we lack, and take what we can for we have little to barter."

"You would not buy the goods if you had all the gold in the world. You much prefer to fight for what you want," said Raum smiling.

Wulfgar burst into laughter. "You do know us well, my lord."

"I know you have the swiftest ships in this part of the world but what of the Moorish fleet in Iberia and southward?"

"Ah, those devils," grinned Wulfgar. "We have met them at sea and even in their own land. We have suffered greatly at their hands and they at ours. We have learned not to raid the heavily armed harbors of the Spanish coast, but to sail on to their native land where they are not so watchful of our attacks." He scratched his beard thoughtfully. "Ah, this land of the black Moors," he continued. "It is a harsh land of desert and scorching sun. It is a land of bloodthirsty men and beautiful hot-blooded women . . . dark women . . . smooth skins, painted eyes and jeweled navels. They sometimes wear small precious stones and ornaments in their noses; their breasts are full and their hips wide . . . their mouths are generous . . ."

"Seeing how taken you are with these women I am surprised at your ever returning home," laughed Raum.

"Why should I stay among such strange folk and suffer their damnable sun when I can take their women home to my own dear land?"

"I should think they would fare poorly in such a frigid clime," mused Raum.

"True, they do not last long but weather has little to do with it," informed the Viking. "They are of a fiery temperament and not easily tamed. You can never trust them. They lead you to believe they welcome their thralldom and then try to push a blade into your ribs. When this does not work they usually kill themselves." He shook his shaggy head and smiled. "Ah, but they are spirited wenches . . . dark, warm skins . . . not the cool cast yours has, friend Raum, but a rosy darkness. That is strange," he said looking closely at Raum's features. "Your cool darkness seems to have warmed and lightened since first we met. Perhaps the talk of women has brought some color to your grim cheeks." Wulfgar laughed and slapped Raum's wide shoulder. The knight laughed also but inwardly wondered at the man's observation.

"What of the great world to the west?" asked Raum changing the subject. "Have you ever sailed there?"

"Of course I have been to Iceland . . . or could it be you speak of Leif's great Vinland?"

"That is what you call the land of the red race?"

"Great thunder," swore Wulfgar, "you do surprise me! How would you know of such things? Many of our ships have gone to this other world but only a few return. Ah, that I could voyage there some day . . . and with you as my companion! We could rule an empire among the red people."

"Perhaps," smiled Raum watching the lein of airborne ravens mingle with some gulls.

Far to the north, on the edge of Jamtland, lay the little village of Bergenklás. The first autumn snow had fallen and the geese had long since left the chilled lakes for warmer nests to the south. The village leader, one Stanfel, stoked the coals in his fireplace where his daughter Helga had put a large pot of stew to simmer. Stanfel leaned to the pot and sniffed critically. Helga was sewing by the window just as her mother had so often done until death had taken her three winters past. The girl was in her sixteenth year and quite pretty but had no thoughts of marriage although several lads of the village tried daily to catch her eye. She felt her purpose in life was to care for her widowed father and this she did with a passion, often near driving poor Stanfel out of his wits.

Bells began pealing from the village watchtower. Helga laid aside her sewing to peer through the frosted window glass.

"What is it?" asked Stanfel straightening from his inspection of the stew.

"I cannot see, Father," replied the girl, "but people are running down the street."

"Fetch me my coat, girl," he said.

She did as he asked and more. She bundled him in

his fur coat and scarf as if he were a child about to go play in the snow.

When Stanfel gained the street he heard shouting from beyond the village limit. It was toward this sound that the people hurried. Stanfel joined them, puffing frosty clouds as he trudged along.

Now, the people of Bergenklas were of a more peaceful nature than those of the coastal settlements where the Viking lords held court. Thus when the herd of reindeer plunged out of the forest bearing goods and riders, the citizens made no hostile move toward them. It was fast apparent that these Fins offered no threat to the people of Bergenklas. They seemed drawn and weary from the ordeal of their journey. Some had the look of weakness that hunger brings.

Among the reindeer was one horse upon which sat a stately youth. 'Twas he that called out the order to halt as the caravan reached the village edge. Having seen this action and the lad's noble bearing, Stanfel rushed forward and addressed him.

"Greetings and welcome to our humble town," said Stanfel bowing his head and doffing his fur trimmed cap.

"Your greetings are welcome, good sir," replied the boy. "To what village have we come?"

"This be Bergenklas, my lad," smiled Stanfel. "Would you be lost?"

"Aye, we are," said the boy. "We have been forced to flee our homeland due to unnatural happenings."

"Pray tell us what these happenings were," urged a villager.

"We come from the kingdom of Thorkuld at Everspring. The lady who rides yonder is Queen Gudren and I am her son Prince Jal. My father, the king, has been slain by a demon in the service of an evil magician whom I have killed. The demon has also perished, I believe, but not before he cursed our fair home and valley. This evil being possessed the power and gift to shake mountains."

The boy stopped in his speech for breath and to check the emotions that rose in his throat. "Our home was a kingdom valley of grass and clear water fed by warm springs. The only real passage from our valley was through a great fjord. 'Twas this the demon brought down. The waters from the warm springs continued to flow, flooding the land and villages for now there was no way to the sea for these waters. In time the last refuge in the valley, Thorkuld's castle, began to take water and we left carrying what we could on our beloved deer. Our journey was made difficult from the first by falling cliffs of ice and snow caused by the temperature of the rising, heated water. Once we were over the mountains that ringed our valley, winter came with savage force and many good people were lost including the queen's own devoted handmaiden."

"Oh, sorrow of sorrows," cried Stanfel assisting the boy out of his saddle. "Come to our meeting hall and rest. We will feed you what we can. Your tale has saddened our hearts for reasons unknown to you, dear prince."

"Our thanks for your kindness, good man, but tell me of what you speak."

"I fear you are mistaken about the demon," said Stanfel shaking his head sadly. " 'Twas several weeks past that strange happenings were reported south of this place. Many were found killed and villages burned, yet no invading army came. The slayings ceased at the southern coast only recently. My guess is that your cruel villain lives and has sailed from our land.

Prince Jal pulled his sword from its scabbard and

shook it above his head crying in a suddenly impassioned voice, "Raum! Raum! I'll see you dead! You will not escape me again! This I vow upon my father's sword."

The fleet of dragon ships rode silently on the darkened sea. Wulfgar watched the inky blackness against the stars that he knew to be Raum. He chewed a piece of salted fish as he walked to where the demon-knight gazed at the sparkling cosmos above.

"Beautiful beyond words, is it not, my friend?" asked Wulfgar.

"That it is," replied Raum quietly. "There is nothing comparable in Netherworld."

"Is this why you come to our world, Lord Raum, to see the stars and the sea?"

"As I have said, Wulfgar, I seek one named Merlin at Arthur's court."

"But why? Are you to take him personally to the other world?"

"That is not my calling."

"I am thinking that wandering about the earth is not your calling either," chuckled Wulfgar.

"I seek not to be mysterious," said Raum. "If I knew what drives me to such lengths I would tell you. I do know that there is something afoot in the world that my Lord Lucifer has seen fit to hold from me. I know that I can no longer be content in the underworld. There is one who lives between our two worlds. He is Merlin. Perhaps he has some answers for me."

"I doubt it, my lord," said Wulfgar, "since you hardly know what questions to ask."

Raum shifted uncomfortably and then said, "I sense land yonder."

"Aye," said Wulfgar, "that would be the isle of

Orkney. A very small isle. Where we go holds more promise. Several of the Briton kings are meeting on the meadows south of the village of Duncansby. They should offer great sport and much booty."

"How would you know of such a meeting?" asked Raum.

"There are those along these coasts who pay tribute to us in the form of bits of information, and we in turn choose not to raid their districts."

In the darkness Wulfgar could see Raum's fiery eyes close in concentration. "I think," said the knight, "that a surprise is being prepared for you this time."

"Speak on," whispered Wulfgar.

" 'Tis true the Scottish kings do gather on the jousting meadow, my captain, but it is more than sport that has brought them and their company to this place. Arthur himself has instructed them to do this for the purpose of enticing you into his trap."

"I have been betrayed by a lowly informer!" cried Wulfgar.

"Be honest," laughed Raum, "Little more could be expected from a traitor."

"Then by the gods," raged the Viking, "the hamlet of Gavinshire will burn tomorrow!"

"That would be the traitor's home?"

"Aye, and Odin grant that he is there when we strike."

The Viking chief began bellowing orders for a change of course. The ravens at roost on the mast and figurehead cried their alarm at the disturbance. "We will hit them with the morning light," shouted Wulfgar.

"Perchance I could add to your plans, friend Wulfgar."

"Speak, my lord," said the Viking.

"If you were to put me and my steed to land near the jousting meet I could occupy these noble kings while you had your way at Gavinshire."

"You could be tricking me," said Wulfgar cautiously, "yet you be not the kind to avoid a good battle. Very well, this sounds promising. Let us plan further."

All had been to chapel, finished a hearty breakfast, donned their colors and armor, and were on the meadow before the sun's rays had burned away the ground mist. Bright tents and stately pavilions stood about the jousting field. Before each hung the shield and standard of some great king or knight. The air was filled with the lusty shouts of eager men and the neighing of excited mounts.

The meadow was traversed by a road that, when leaving the northern part, continued a short way to the town of Duncansby. Where its course led southward, it was lost in a thick wood and the rolling hills beyond. It was from this direction that most had come with their retinues of servants and beasts of burden.

On the western edge of the game field was a pavilion more magnificent than all the rest. Here the pennants and standard of Arthur moved gently to the morning winds. Squires in rich clothing assisted knights with armor and weapons as young pages hurried about the encampment with tasks and messages from the gathered kings. These were the gallant kings who now gave their allegiance to Arthur Pendragon, King of all Britons.

By the time the sun was a quarter way up the sky many a lance had been splintered and many a knight had found himself placed rudely on the ground. Back and forth went the charging mounts as the air filled with shouts of encouragement from the onlookers. Each time the trump sounded, two knights on festooned chargers would enter the field to face each other in the skill of combat. Yet if one were well-schooled in the ways of jousting, one might perceive that although the fighting was lusty there was a certain lack, for none of these worthy knights suffered wounds of a great and serious nature.

Although Arthur was in his armor, he had not taken to the field as had not several others gathered about him. Arthur sat before his pavilion in conversation with some of the great knights of his court. There was Sir Gawain and the ever-present Lancelot. Near at hand were Sir Kay and a king of Orkney who had pledged his loyalty to Arthur. This king was called Lot, and it was he who had helped the Britons to prepare and ward off the attacking of those Viking kings who would pledge loyalty to no man. The king from the island of Orkney and even a king from Ireland stood close by as if awaiting some sign from Arthur.

" 'Twould seem, sire," Gawain was saying to Arthur, "our friend in Gavinshire had faulty news."

"The day is still young," replied the king. "If no assault has come to Duncansby by midday we shall have our tournament in earnest and fight the Norsemen another time."

"Hold!" said Sir Kay raising a gauntleted hand, "I seem to be hearing a pounding of earth in yonder woods."

"Aye, that it is," said Arthur standing and signaling the two knights upon the field to cease their contest.

The heavy pounding grew louder and out from the lane through the forest rode a gigantic knight upon a steed unlike any seen by those gathered there. Both the knight's armor and the monstrous horse were the color of a moonless night. The stranger's face was hidden by his dark-winged helmet and none had seen such a device as that upon his shield. He rode onto the field unchallenged and came straight way to where Arthur watched. Nor did he dismount when the great charger stopped before the king. His raised, mailed hand was his only greeting.

"Welcome, sir knight," said Arthur somewhat uncertainly. "Have you come to join our sport?"

"Indeed I have," came the knight's loud and heavy voice.

"I do not recognize your shield's strange emblem," said Arthur. "By what name are you called and from what land do you ride?"

"I am of noble birth, sire, and am called Raum. My land is far from your fair Camelot. None of your brave knights have visited my realm and few shall, I fear. Its name would mean little to you. But I came to challenge the best of the famed Knights of the Round Table."

Sir Kay laughed loudly and said, "I and my two companions, Sir Gawain and Lancelot of the Lake, all bear such distinction. Forgive me, sir, but humility is not a strong virtue of mine I fear."

A laugh came from the black winged helmet causing feelings of disquiet among those who heard it. "Then let me test you first," said the dark warrior.

"Done," replied Kay eagerly and took his helmet from his squire.

Sir Kay, arrayed in bright silks and mounted on a fine dapple courser, took his place in the north of the meadow. As the stranger wheeled about in the south field he offered much contrast to Kay for he seemed a forbidding dark shadow. Those who watched wondered at the large number of ravens about the meadow now.

Sir Gawain leaned to Arthur's ear and said, "I do hope the ravens are not some dire omen."

Arthur made no reply but signaled the youth with the trumpet to sound the knights to combat.

The very earth trembled as the great black charger rushed to close with the dapple. Sir Kay leaned forward behind his bright shield, his lance well-couched at full tilt. Lord Raum's spear, it was noted, was much longer than Sir Kay's as the two came together. Thus the fair knight was lifted from his saddle before his lance had touched the dark shield. The dapple cried shrilly and fell beneath the great black to be savagely trampled. Although Kay fell with broken ribs, he did fall clear of the crushing hooves.

Arthur quickly signaled and the trumpet called for Raum's withdrawal which he honored and returned to his place in the south.

"I shall teach this oaf a lesson sure," cried Lancelot making ready to mount and ride into the meadow.

"Hold!" ordered the king. "I fear more takes place here than is quickly seen, fair knight. Until all is clear, I would have you stay and be on guard for the Viking lord may be a part of this."

"Then I?" asked Gawain.

"Stay you also," said Arthur sternly, "for Kay's place has already been taken by another." This was true for now a knight of Lot's court saluted Raum and made ready to charge.

Once more the earth trembled and quaked as the mounts rushed to meet. Once more Raum's spear outreached the other's and the results were much the same as before. The knight, Sir Loadice, fell clear as had Kay, but his horse fell screaming beneath the black charger and so tangled itself in the monster's legs that

Raum found himself crashing to earth not far from Loadice.

Now Loadice was a young and agile knight. He gained his feet some time before Raum and ran toward the dark knight with drawn sword. Raum's big hand had just touched his sword hilt when it was struck a stinging blow. His other arm, however, was raised high, ax in hand. Before Loadice could recover his stance, the ax fell with lightning speed and all could hear the metal of his bright helmet tear asunder followed by the death cry of brave Loadice.

The dark knight then did that which would never be honored wherever knighthood flourished. He hacked the young knight's head from its body and threw it, blood streaming, at the feet of Arthur. All about the field stood in horror and drew blades to avenge this outrage. It would be difficult to say how many might have died had not a shout of challenge rung out from the northern end of the meadow.

"You, sir, are a coward and dishonor all knighthood. Put your foul self onto your horse again that I may give you the undeserved honor of a man's death."

Raum turned at the sound of the young, emotion-filled voice. Two knights sat their mounts facing him. One had his helmet beneath his arm and was fair handsome to see, but it was not he who had spoken, but his companion. Raum's red eyes closed tight at the brilliance of the challenging knight's armor. His armor gleamed white as the sun itself as did his shield, yet it bore a tall red cross as its device. His visor was opened to reveal a flawless face with light blue eyes. Raum turned away and would not look upon these fairest of knights. None can say how much blood would have soaked the meadow that day had Arthur not then spoken.

"Come forward, Lord Raum," ordered the king.

The demon-knight did as he was bid and raised his visor as he bowed before the king.

Arthur and those who could see Raum's evil features were shocked at the hate-filled eyes. "Please," said Arthur, "tell me if I have wronged you in some way that you should soil the very name of chivalry before us."

"Forgive me, sire," said Raum with pretended humility, "for I did forget my location. Such methods of battle are quite common and acceptable in the land from which I come."

"What has brought you to this place?" asked the king.

"I come to speak to one of your court, sire," replied Raum.

"Who do you seek?"

"Merlin, Your Highness."

"For what purpose?"

"That is not clear even to me, Majesty. When might I speak with the magician?"

"Alas, you are too late, Lord Raum. Merlin has vanished and there are only women's tales as to his whereabouts."

"What woman tells these tales?" asked Raum.

"My sister, Lady Morgan Le Fey. I can tell you little of what she might say as we have not been closely knit of late. Yonder is King Lot, her husband, but he too is estranged from her and could tell you less. The Lady Le Fey is not beloved of our people. She is given to practicing the darker rites of sorcery. I would caution you to never travel to her castle, as she has men-at-arms that are quite bloodthirsty and she welcomes no one."

"Have you not sought the magician?" asked Raum, displeased with this news.

"Merlin has left us without word before . . . perhaps for not so long a time, but I am not overly concerned. I pray only that the kind wizard has not been carried away by some foul being of his own conjuration."

"I thank you, sire, for all your information and would ask just one more question. Where is Lady Le Fey's castle?"

"Very well, somber knight," said Arthur showing his irritation. "You have been warned and the responsibility shall not be mine. Hers is the castle Dolorous Garde that stands in the marshland beyond Alder Wood."

"My thanks for your words of caution. Your manners make me sorrow that I killed your brave kinsman." Raum paused and smiled at Arthur saying, "In my land, sire, one pitches the head of the loser of the contest at the feet of the one he most respects and would serve. My hope is that you can see fit to understand and forgive my error."

"I have always striven to be kind and fair. I shall believe for now that you acted from ignorance," said Arthur frowning, "but I would urge you to leave this kingdom soon for if you were again to forget yourself, 'twould be most hard to forgive."

"I shall take this warning to heart, sire, and tarry no longer than is necessary," said Raum bowing deeply, a crooked smile playing on his lips. He turned to go but hesitated.

"There is something more?" asked Arthur making no attempt to hide his displeasure.

"Two things make me curious about your jousting here today, noble king. There is no sign of your ladies and I have been told they fair flock to such events. The second is the identity of those two knights who had challenged me when you halted the games."

"A clever observation about the ladies, Sir Raum," replied Arthur, "and 'tis true there are none here to-day. We had been warned that the northern hordes would attack Duncansby close by. The tournament was a ruse to have the best fighting men here to stand them off and perchance to put an end to their raids for a time."

"Ah, 'tis as I thought," smiled Raum revealing his fangs, "and what of the two fair knights?"

"The one in blue is Sir Percival, a standard of chivalry and knighthood to all men. The one that stands in brightest armor is Sir Galahad the Pure, the fairest and most saintly of knights."

"My thanks again for your kind answers," said Raum. "Those two do interest me strangely. 'Twould be the pity to slay such fellows. I therefore beg your generosity in asking that you order them to vow upon their honor to bear no sword against me. Do this thing and I shall tell you of a secret that will hold great interest for you."

"I have felt you harbored some secret, Lord Raum. So be it," said Arthur standing and pointing to where Percival and Galahad sat their mounts. "I pray you good knights to vow peace between you and this stranger in that you shall never draw your blades against him."

The young knights conversed together for a moment and then placed their right hands over their breasts and said, "It is done, sire."

"And now, my mysterious fellow," said Arthur turning to Raum, "you have a secret to reveal?"

"Indeed I have," said Raum stepping back and

placing his hand on the black steed's saddle. "This raid
you spoke of . . ." he swung his heavily muscled body
onto the animal's back ". . . I fear it was not Duncansby that has been visited by Viking guests this day."

"What is your meaning?" demanded Arthur.

"I would hope that none here have homes in that
place called Gavinshire for it has been burned and
plundered even as we jousted this fine morning."

A loud cry of alarm went up around the gathering.
Arthur held up his hand for silence and then spoke,
his eyes wide with rage, "How do you come by such
knowledge?"

" 'Twas the selfsame Vikings you spoke of that
brought me to your shores last night," said Raum smiling. "Our plan was that I should keep you entertained
until they had their fill of fun at Gavinshire."

"Obstinate hulk!" shouted Gawain leaping to
his mount, only to have Raum's lance smash him back
to earth.

Arthur shouted to the others, "To the horses! Forget this foulest of knights for now. 'Tis Gavinshire that
needs us."

Although Arthur himself had ordered no further
contact with Raum there were a few who could not
resist one charge at the dark warrior before riding off
the field with the others. Each regretted this breach
quickly when they found themselves unhorsed and
under the pounding hooves of Raum's great steed.
The pages and other servantfolk who remained behind
to strike the various tents and pavilions stood in horror
as the great black mount stamped and cavorted over the
fallen bodies rendering them to a pulp. They heard the
dark knight's awful laughter as he rode from the field
upon his blood-spattered horse and went northward
toward Duncansby.

Village mayor Stanfel was glad he had insisted upon the queen and her son taking lodging at his house until such time the lady might be strong enough to travel again. Their presence diverted much of the unwanted attention which his daughter showered on him to the point of suffocation. Helga now busied herself nursing Queen Gudren and feeding Prince Jal. Stanfel noted with a degree of satisfaction that the boy did not ignore her attentions. Although the lad had given his age as just having passed his thirteenth birthday, he looked all of twenty, but of course he and his mother had seen much of life these past months. Stanfel could see the boy had matured by the way his eyes played over the mounds of Helga's full breasts. He wondered if the prince had made advances toward the buxom girl in his absence. Well, what matter? At least Helga did not constantly fuss at him about his food, clothing, drinking and taking walks in the forest when it snowed.

Stanfel wrapped a scarf about his scrawny neck in preparation to go on some errand in the village. When Helga entered the room and began nagging him about hooking his collar he asked her, "Why are you not attending the queen and her son?"

"Queen Gudren sleeps and the prince has gone into the village," she replied as she fastened the collar.

"Why has he gone out? Did he tell you?"

"Of course not," she said sharply. "You do not question a prince's every move."

"He has seemed restless these past days," commented Stanfel. "He has plied me with questions of the reports of the killings to the south. I fear the boy's hatred for the demon will destroy him."

Stanfel had just stepped into the snow-covered street when he saw Prince Jal. The boy sat upon his horse and led another he had apparently purchased at the village stable. He rode at a good pace toward Stanfel.

"Hail, my prince," called the mayor. "What brings you out on such a day? We are sure to have more snow before the day is through."

Jal pulled his mount to a halt before his benefactor. "I make ready to leave this happy town," said the boy.

"But what is this you say?" exclaimed Stanfel.

"Delay your business in the village and return with me to your home where I may bid you and your lovely daughter farewell in proper manner," said the prince with a sad smile.

Stanfel walked behind the two horses, politely protesting the lad's decision. Upon reaching the mayor's house Jal called his mother and Helga to join them before the fireplace in the main room.

"What news do you have, my son?" asked Gudren.

"I have talked to a man that is newly returned from the south. He tells me one Wulfgar has sailed with a war fleet for the land of the Britons. I feel it certain that Raum would not pass such an opportunity. I have purchased a pack animal and shall follow the devil in his search for the magician."

Helga fell at the blond boy's feet crying.

His hand smoothed her hair as he said, "Do me good service, sweet girl, and care for my mother, the queen, in my absence. I will return for you both if it be Odin's will."

"Ah, that I had the love and strength of character to command you to stay," said Queen Gudren, her eyes wide with hate and terror, "but I do not. Forgive me, Jal, but I pray only that you kill him! Kill him! Kill him!" She collapsed into her son's arms sobbing.

Raum sat his saddle at ease surveying the town from his place on the hill near the forest. The ravens perched among the branches watching him with interest. Beyond the town to the east lay the sea and upon its sparkling surface came the Viking fleet just as he and Wulfgar had planned. A bell began ringing in the village. Raum smiled his satisfaction. There would be no knights rushing to Duncansby's aid this day. He wondered, however, if there might not be archers placed within the town walls.

The dark, steel-clad giant breathed deeply, his red eyes flaring. He stretched forth his hand and chanted three strange words. A great rumbling began all about him sending the ravens to flight. The earth rolled beneath the hoofs of his mount but the agile animal kept its balance well. The trembling increased as it approached the walls of·Duncansby. Soon the earth was rent with fissures and the walls began to fall to rubble. Cries and shouting could be heard from those caught in the falling wood and stone. Raum noted the large number of archer's platforms that were exposed momentarily before plunging earthward with their occupants.

The quake had generated large waves offshore and the Norsemen were hard pressed to keep their ships afloat and off the rocks along the shore. Once the sea had settled the Viking warriors streamed ashore and ran toward the shattered town.

From his place on the hill Raum could hear the sounds of battle. He eased his mount into a slow pace watching for any who might attempt escape. In a ditch, newly formed by the quake, Raum spied a head bobbing along at an uneven gait. He rode to the brink of the depression and stared at the man scurrying through the dirt.

The man was not young and wore the cassock of a priest. When his eyes caught sight of the black-armored warrior above him he cried out and fell to his knees praying. Raum made no move toward the man. He began to laugh his cynical amusement at the sight of the pitiful fellow. The priest stopped his prayers, his eyes becoming slits as he glared back at his intimidator.

"I would guess you be Satan himself," said the man loudly. "I have always said that if ever we should meet 'twould be my pleasure to spit into your eye. Could you move a bit closer, foul creature? Your present place would tax my poor strength and spittal."

Raum's laughter boomed over the little man's head. "Well said, priest," said the hellish warrior, "but you pay me too large a compliment. I am only an earl, not a king."

"But you hail from the same kingdom?" cried the priest.

"That would be so," chuckled Raum, "but tell me, my brave man of peace, where did you think you were off to?"

"To fetch those who would send you back to where you belong!" shouted the trembling cleric.

Raum lowered his spear to the brave man and said, "Hold to my lance, little man, that I may lift you from your earthen hole." He hoisted the man aloft on his lance and set him roughly on the grass. The priest lay breathing heavily as Raum dismounted and removed his helmet. He knelt to speak to the churchman and was met with a shower of saliva in his face.

No longer smiling Raum wiped his face on the man's robe. "You make it difficult for me to choose a fitting death for you," growled the knight.

"Do your worst!" shouted the priest.

"You think your God will save you?"

"He did that long ago," retorted the priest. "You may do what you will with my mortal body, but you shall never subdue my soul."

"Why do you talk such nonsense when you are about to die?" asked Raum in exasperation. "I was mistaken in thinking you brave, you are only a fool." The priest's lips moved in soundless prayer. "If your God has already saved your soul why do you continue to pray?" sneered Raum.

"I do not pray for myself," said the priest. "I pray for those dying in the town today and . . . for you."

"What?" roared the knight, aghast. "What form has your madness taken now?"

"You were quite correct in pointing out the futility in praying for myself for there is no need. The soul of one such as you is in greater need and the salvation of such a soul would be of benefit to all of mankind."

"Still your tongue!" shouted Raum raising his hand to strike the priest.

The little man closed his eyes and continued his prayers. Even when metal clanked and the great horse stamped about him he continued his holy rites. Only when the pounding hoofbeats were fading in the distance did he open his eyes.

Amid the flame and ruin that had been proud Duncansby, stood Wulfgar directing his men in the sacking of what remained. Those citizens who had not been put to the sword now fled to open country. The Viking chief's attention was suddenly drawn to where a part of the city wall now fell to rubble. He could see a very tall figure standing there in the smoke and dust. Wulfgar shivered visibly as he recognized the diabolical knight he had brought to these shores. He watched, fascinated, as the dark swordsman moved among the fallen defenders striking with his war ax all those who showed life. The great, menacing figure made its way to where the village church and bell tower stood with little evidence of damage. Raum shattered the door with his gory ax and entered the building. Wulfgar could hear the knight's great voice within shouting his impassioned curses. Cracks appeared in the stonework masonry and when Raum emerged, the tower and walls began folding in upon themselves. The whole ruined pile then burst into flame and smoke. Wulfgar thanked Odin silently that this horror in armor was no longer in his beloved Norway.

"You permitted some to escape!" stormed Raum as he walked to where Wulfgar stood.

"Only children and a few old people," explained the Viking.

"I do not understand your delicacy in battle," fumed Raum. "I had thought you a man with whom I had much in common. Sad to say I was in error."

"You must realize, my lord, you come from a country where evil and brutality have been carried to a perfection. How could we mortals achieve that which gods have done?"

"Ha!" exploded Raum into sudden laughter. "What you intended as evasive wit might very well be true."

"And where do you go now, my lord?" asked Wulfgar relaxing.

"With you, of course," said Raum becoming serious once more.

The Viking chieftain took a step backward cautiously. "No, my lord, you shall not return with me. Already too many Norsemen have died at your hands. Now it may be my time to the same, but I will not take you back to Norway."

"I said nothing of Norway," replied Raum calmly. "You will take me south to where a castle stands, to a place called Dolorous Garde."

"That accursed place! I know it well. Several of my men lie dead in the murky water that surrounds it. 'Tis no place for any man . . . yet for you, my lord, it might be fitting." He noted that the men were loading the last of their plundered wealth onto the ships. He turned back to Raum saying, "Very well, friend Raum, we shall sail south for you before returning home. We must show our gratitude for this day's work."

The Viking raiders rested that night in a secluded cove on the isle of Orkney before continuing southward along the Scottish coast. The cove had high cliffs on three sides thus making it relatively safe to have cooking fires at night. None would see their light save from the open sea and these men feared no one upon the water.

After the evening meal Wulfgar joined Raum on shore where he lay resting beneath some low scrub trees. "A pleasant night to end a profitable day," sighed the Viking as he sat down on a nearby stone. "Would you be wanting a woman tonight, my lord? We have many on the larger ships."

Raum made no reply.

"Your thirst for blood today surprised even me, Lord Raum. I found your destruction of the church most puzzling. Do you feel so threatened by these people's religion? I cannot see where it is in any way superior to our own, at least today it helped them naught. What provoked you into such vengeance?"

"I met a priest from the church outside the village.

'Twas he that provoked me. He would not react and behave as men should. He was the first man I have met that . . ."

"Yes, my lord?"

"He did confuse me so!" sighed Raum.

"Was his death a slow one?" asked Wulfgar.

"I . . . I saw no need to kill him."

"What?" exclaimed the Viking leaping to his feet. "You storm at me for permitting a few harmless ones to escape, while letting this milksop priest go free after putting you in such a rage that you try to kill and destroy everything in the village? I thank Odin that we are not more similar, my friend, for I think you are a fool at times and that one day it will cost you your life."

"Do not test my patience further," growled Raum.

Wulfgar, without another word tramped off into the darkness toward the ships where the cries of women and the laughter of men could be heard.

Winter's first storm came in a fury from the sea at daybreak. Although Raum was more than anxious to be on his way south, he knew Wulfgar spoke wisely when he said that no ship could sail until the storm had calmed. Soon the ships lay encrusted with ice. The men built what shelters they could among the rocks and sat about fires wrapped in heavy blankets and skins. On the fourth day the storm moved out to sea once more and shafts of sunlight streaked the windswept sky.

"We sail," announced Wulfgar to Raum that morning. "We take only one ship. The others will wait here in safety from the weather and Arthur's vengeance."

Thus it was that late one evening Raum readied the livery of the great horse tethered to the mast. Wulfgar had indicated that they would go ashore under the cover of night. The crew would remain aboard while their chief would land with Raum and guide him to the path to Dolorous Garde. The ravens could be heard in the darkened forest along the shore. Their calls cheered Raum's cold heart and his spirits were high as he followed Wulfgar, leading his horse ashore through the icy surf.

"Yonder lies Alder Wood, my lord," said the Norseman. "We may build a fire there if you desire it. Few come this way and with good reason. The Lady Le Fey consorts with creatures not of this world and enjoys the pain and death of others above all else."

Raum laughed saying, "One might describe you in similar terms, my bloody friend."

Wulfgar showed his displeasure at Raum's comparison by refusing the knight's invitation to ride with him upon the fabulous steed. They had not gone far into the dense forest before the Viking indicated they should build a fire and wait for dawn's first light before approaching the castle. "It is unwise to confront evil creatures in the dark for it is from darkness that such things gain their strength," he stated.

"I assure you," laughed Raum, "I shall be as strong in the morning as I am now in darkness."

"I spoke not of you, my lord, as you are not the ordinary devil one encounters."

"Oh? And have you encountered many devils, Wulfgar?"

"Indeed I have," stated the Viking without embarrassment. "Many have I seen in this very region."

Chuckling, Raum dismounted and helped Wulfgar gather wood for the fire. In no time at all a cozy warmth filled the camp. Wulfgar dozed tiredly before the fire as Raum lay with his back against a large moss-covered oak, pitching bits of meat to the ravens. Suddenly his hand froze in midair as he listened. The ravens became still as did the big red-eyed charger. In the next moment the dark birds had risen into the night air crying their alarm. "Wulfgar!" shouted Raum pulling his sword free of its scabbard.

The Viking's sword was in his hand before his eyes were fully opened. Arrows made whining noises about him and then the sickening little sounds of their impact was heard among the trees nearby. He was blinded by the fire's light and followed Raum's example of leaping back out of the glow and into the cover of bramble and darkness. Voices shouted all about them now and the arrows continued to sing their deathly song overhead. He could not see the dark warrior but felt he was not far to his left. Raum's great horse cried out and charged into the forest. Wulfgar could also hear the screams of those who were unfortunately in the monster horse's path.

Behind him came the sounds of another horse trampling the crisp leaves of autumn past. The horse cried out as did its rider and Wulfgar knew Lord Raum had found his first victim of the night, but their location was immediately set upon by charging men-at-arms, one of which tripped over the Viking's fur-wrapped feet. Wulfgar hacked at the man's neck with his blade but still a cry of discovery escaped. Two more bodies hurled at him and there must have been a third behind him for a sharp pain exploded in his thick skull. Before total darkness claimed him, he saw Raum near the fire battling four armored knights. "Arthur's men," he murmured and fell.

Raum knew he had the choice of being trampled or facing the man at sword's point, thus he sprang upon the rider revealing his place of hiding. He never

saw the man's face as he cut his throat but he did feel
the chain mail and breastplate. The man was a
knight!

"Here, friend!" called a voice behind him. "Come
meet your just death!"

Raum leaped clear of the tangled undergrowth and
found himself facing the knight of Arthur's court called
Gawain and three others like him. It was then that a
shout came from the wood and Raum knew Wulfgar
was discovered.

"Step into the light and do fair battle," taunted
Gawain.

"With a shout of rage Raum plunged into the four
knights with such force that one lost his sword arm
while another fell howling into the fire. Gawain and
his remaining companion separated to each side of
the demon-knight. "You wasted little time coming
here, my lord," said Raum to the famous knight,
"from where I saw you last."

" 'Twas Lot that recalled your inquiries of Dolorous
Garde. We guessed you traveled by ship with your
bloody Vikings and that the storm would cause you
delay enough for us to meet you here."

"Well thought," smiled Raum cynically. All about
the clearing men began appearing with sword and
bow. Two men carried the limp body of Wulfgar into
the firelight and dumped it rudely on the ground.

"Do you yield, my lord?" asked Gawain.

"Alas, I cannot do as you ask, good knight, for my
blade has not had its fill of blood this day." So saying
Raum pitched low to the ground and sliced the ankle
joints of Gawain's companion. Arthur's noble knight
rushed upon him only to have Raum's heavy foot
smash into his face. The demon-knight's sword shot
upward and found a place to enter Gawain's armor

near the shoulder. It withdrew in a shower of crimson. A shout of dismay went up from the gathered warriors as Gawain fell to the leaf-strewn earth.

"Together, men!" shouted one, but before they could act the unholy knight reached into the campfire and began hurling blazing logs their way. The men stepped lively to avoid the fiery missiles but only to find the undergrowth of the forest now ignited. As the trees caught and the flames leaped higher the men began milling about in confused terror.

Raum selected them two and three at a time for his ax to fell like trees. Some ran screaming, seeking escape through the forest that was now an inferno. Raum picked the fallen Viking from the ground. Holding the big man in his arms, the sinister warrior walked into the exploding madness that had been Alder Wood.

As Raum made his way through the forest he watched for some sign of his horse but soon concluded the beast had fled the scene completely. Once he had gained the forest edge he looked back to where the night sky shone red with fire and smoke. Against the lurid light could be seen the wheeling, dark shapes of ravens. He adjusted the weight of the Viking over his wide shoulder and trudged on toward the sea.

He had not gone far however until looming against the rising moon was a knight upon a charger with lance at full tilt. "Do you choose to pray before you die?" asked the knight in a youthful voice.

"Who challenges me?" asked Raum dropping Wulfgar to the soft turf.

"Percival of the Round Table, my lord!"

Raum sucked in his breath between bared fangs. "Have you forgotten your vow to your king so soon?"

"Nay, I have not. The vow was that I not bear my

sword against you, treacherous knight, but said nothing of my spear, mace or ax."

"I felt you a fair knight above all else," protested Raum. "Now I find you bending truth to fit your needs!"

" 'Tis my own overlarge conscience that forbids me using my sword to slay you for fear of doing that which my savior Jesus would not want. Why do you act the coward now when less than a week past you challenged the greatest knights of the realm?"

"Begone, fair knight, for I too have such feelings and fears though I know little of your Christian God. As you might suspect such things are not widely discussed in Netherworld."

"You miss my meaning, sir. My concern is to not kill you with my sword but I fully intend to kill you. You do make me curious and want to question you further but that is not my purpose. Before you die, however, tell of yonder blaze in Alder Wood."

Raum's old sinister smile returned to his evil features. " 'Tis only a fire to roast your fellow knight Sir Gawain who lies wounded there by my hand."

The young knight shouted an oath and dug his heels deep into his mount's ribs sending the beast forward in a mad charge. The lance he bore picked Raum's heavy body from the ground and flung it aside. Percival continued his impassioned ride into the burning forest calling Gawain's name.

Dark-red blood spilled from Raum's side as he stood and lifted Wulfgar who was moaning and regaining his senses. The two now supported one another as they went unsteadily toward where they guessed the ship to be. Wulfgar showed concern for Raum's wound and asked how he had received it. The

dark knight would only say that it was one of
Arthur's knights that had dealt the blow.

Upon reaching the cove where they had landed,
they found only two of their men and they were quite
dead. The ship was gone and these had been its
sentries. Both Raum and Wulfgar sank to the rocky
earth to rest.

"My men would not leave if they thought I lived,"
moaned Wulfgar.

"I sense they are not far," said Raum closing his
eyes, "perhaps just beyond that point of land in the
darkness there."

"Ah, that would be their way," said Wulfgar taking
a small signal horn from his leather girdle and putting
it to his lips. He sounded his call twice before it was
answered from out of the blackness that still clung
to the sea. He leaned back in the soft grass and said,
"That accursed magician Merlin is the one that told
Arthur where he might find us . . . ah, the ship
comes."

Soon they were aboard ship once more and moving out to sea. The crew quickly related to their
chieftain how there had come a great shower of arrows from the high shore while they were awaiting
Wulfgar's return. Being unable to see the enemy or
their number, they had retired to the safety of the sea.

"You see, friend Raum," smiled the old Viking,
"they are good men."

Before the sun had set they entered the inlet at
Orkney. Those ships that were still afloat were badly
burned. The dragonheads and masts of the others rose
starkly from the waves. The tide was awash with
corpses. There was no sign of life. None of Wulfgar's
crew spoke as their ship glided into what would

never again be considered a safe haven for Nordic ships.

"How were they discovered?" exploded Wulfgar. "Is the treasure at the bottom of the inlet or has it been carried away? Were there no prisoners taken? Put into shore!"

"You think it wise, my friend?" asked Raum.

"Indeed I do, Lord Raum, for here is where we shall part company. We must sail for home while still there is one ship left. As I told you before I cannot give you passage back to Norway."

"Perhaps you are right, Wulfgar. Our luck seems to have turned against us."

"Once back in my beloved homeland I shall think back on these days, my friend," said Wulfgar slapping Raum's shoulder, "and I will recall you were the greatest warrior of them all. The pain of our loss shall soften with time and perhaps we shall even find ourselves in the thick of battle together again, side by side."

"That would be my wish also, Wulfgar," said the knight.

They left Raum with provisions on the shore, then headed out to open sea. He watched until the sail was lost from view, then lifted his bundles and climbed to the top of the surrounding rocks. He began his trek southward but had not gone far when he noticed a movement in some brambles close by. He moved with caution but as he drew near saw that it was not needed. A wounded man lay in the thicket, his eyes open but unseeing. The blood that covered his clothing had dried and Raum surmised he had been there for some time. The man was a Viking from the lost ships. Raum could tell the man held to life by only a thread.

Kneeling beside the fallen Norseman, Raum asked, "How did this happen?"

The man's eyes flickered in search of Raum's face. His lips parted and in a rasping voice he said, "Only a lad. A lad and a king."

"What king?" asked Raum.

"The King of Orkney just returned from the games at Duncansby. So filled with hate and vengeance . . ."

"How did he discover the ships?"

"The boy . . . the Finnish prince. He saw our fires as his ship passed us at night. He put in and warned the king."

"How do you know this?"

"The lad was there enjoying the bloody view. They thought me dead . . . I heard them talking. 'Tis the monster knight he seeks. I must warn Wulfgar . . ."

"How was the Finnish lad called?" asked Raum quietly.

"A prince he was . . . Jal . . ." sighed the man with his last breath.

Raum stood clenching his big fists, his eyes glowing in the fading light. He heard his winged companions high in the murky sky. "Jal! Jal!" he said through tight lips. "I pray to all the gods that our paths do cross once more for I shall never rest until I have plucked your body apart one limb at a time!"

The enraged warrior spent the next several hours trudging toward what he felt would be the island's nearest shore to the Scottish coast. He found a fisher's hovel at water's edge with a boat tied to its crude dock. Raum did not hesitate when he reached the humble door. One blow from his mighty fist sent it flying inward. The occupant of the shed was a skinny fellow in rags, not young anymore. Upon seeing his door suddenly destroyed and then the awful countenance of Raum appear out of the night, the poor man fainted dead away. Raum ignored him and left him where he lay. The diabolical knight sat before the fisherman's fire and ate the man's supper.

As Raum stared into the flames they flickered brightly and the face of Asteroth, his superior in the underworld, appeared smiling, as was his habit.

"Your adventures do not seem to go well, Lord Raum," said Asteroth. "Would you be ready to admit to your folly now and return to your proper place?"

"What has happened only makes my staying here more dear to me. Your badgering, I might add, makes my resistance more determined," replied Raum.

"You will continue to seek the Druid?" asked Asteroth. "All my efforts with the delaying storm and leading Arthur's men to you has been for naught?"

"You take too much credit, my lord," smirked Raum. "This be the season for storms here, they need no supernatural assistance. As for Arthur's men finding us, 'tis I that must take that credit. You are right in one respect, however, I am a fool but I am learning."

"You are losing!" shouted Asteroth in exasperation. "Each day you become more human. Can you not see it? You bled from a spear wound and more and more you are becoming subject to pain. Even your bluish skin has lightened and warmed in hue. Soon your magical gifts shall begin to fail you. What then, Earl Raum?"

"I feel all this necessary if I am to find the answers I seek."

"Beware then!" raged Asteroth. "Beware of that which makes man most vulnerable, my lord, for surely it lies in your path!"

Before Raum could question the master demon further, he faded into the flames and was gone. The dusky knight stood and threw the dish, from which he had been eating, against the wall smashing it. He stepped over the unconscious fisherman and strode from the poor dwelling to where the boat was tied. Out there in the fog and darkness lay Scotland.

PART 3

Three Elven Ladies

DURING THE NIGHT the snowfall ended and when the sun's first rays struck the high towers of Camelot the sky was all a flawless blue. The colored pennants upon these towers set the mood of the day as they fluttered gaily in the breeze. Young boys were the first to appear and began pelting one another with snowballs. They were then joined by young maids who seemed intent on erecting a monumental figure of snow. By midmorning, the lords and ladies of Camelot had also joined them and the atmosphere was truly festive.

There was laughing and singing too as two heavy draft animals drew a large sledge among the revelers. Riding on the low vehicle were two knights and a bevy of fine ladies. Another knight rode his mount close by and called to those who lounged beside the ladies.

"Lazy wastrels, will your wounds never heal or is it you much prefer your present company?"

"Do not annoy us with your taunts, Gareth," responded one of those upon the sledge.

His fellow beside him added, "Gawain and I both will challenge you to a joust before Candlemas since the kind ministrations of Sir Pelleas' dear wife Lady Nimue and the gracious Lady Viviene are making our recovery near miraculous."

Sir Gareth stood in his stirrups and hooted his laughter. "If the two ladies have done so well with their nursing, Sir Kay, why do so many fair maids feel compelled to give assistance to the healing of a few cracked ribs?"

One of the ladies beside the ailing knights spoke then. "Be off with you, Sir Gareth, if you have no other charity to offer these poor knights."

Gareth laughed and doffed his fur cap to the women. "I meant no offense, Lady Nimue. All was said in jest as well my fellows know. My apology to you and Lady Viviene."

Another of the women, a dark-haired and singularly beautiful lady all wrapped in gray furs, smiled to Gareth and said, "Your ill manners are pardoned, sir, but frolic not here when you could do good service for the king."

"How so, Lady Viviene?" asked Gareth.

"Beyond where the road turns yonder into the forest comes the king's own sister Lady Morgan Le Fey. 'Twould seem fitting if some from this fair court did escort her."

Gareth could see no sign of Lady Le Fey's approach but he knew well the magical perception of Lady Viviene and was not surprised when a line of armored riders emerged from the distant forest. Gareth did, however, dislike this lady's coming for the day had been one of high spirits and he knew that this would end now, due to the long-standing resentment between the king and his half-sister.

As Gareth rode to meet the Queen of Dolorous Garde's company, those sporting in the snow ceased their merry chatter upon seeing the approaching retinue. Sir Gawain on the snow sledge leaned to Lady Viviene and said, "Would your mistress be coming to fetch you, my lady?"

"I hardly think it so, my lord," said Viviene. "She gave me free leave to come assist Lady Nimue in the relieving of your afflictions. 'Twould seem she wishes to see the king."

When Arthur's fair queen, Guinevere, was told of Lady Morgan Le Fey's arrival, she bristled and sent a message to the king that she was not feeling at all well and would not be able to receive the Queen of Dolorous Garde. The reasons that stirred such unfriendly feelings in both the the king and queen against Lady Le Fey were commonly known.

Arthur had once held his half-sister in the highest regard and trust until his discovery that she harbored a hateful jealously of him, and that she plotted to steal his sacred sword and leave him vulnerable to his enemies. He also disapproved of her attempt to murder her husband. But Arthur was a loving man by nature and although he would never trust this woman again, he did make her welcome at court as was the way of chivalry. He assumed her dark ways came from ancestry, for it was said, and Arthur never denied it, that his sister's father had been a devil. Now this is not to say Arthur believed her to be the daughter of a real devil, but he greatly suspected that she, like the other Ladies of the Lake, to be of elven folk.

To fully understand who the elven folk really were, we must go backwards in time to before there had been any invasions by Angles, Saxons or Ro-

mans. Already these isles were peopled by a strange
and powerful folk. Their language was unlike any
other, yet even today in Wales, traces of this tongue
can still be heard. They called themselves Mabden
(The People) and theirs was a religion of enchant-
ments and magical worship. They were never completely Christianized by the Roman occupation and
hid from their would-be conquerors in the wilds
of the great heath. Thus it was they came to be known
as heathens and their worship held to be evil and
contemptible.

In an age much later than our present story,
the last of the elven people, who also were called
Prytains, vanished from their last stronghold in the
north of Scotland. Legends of elves and other
magical creatures have come down to us due to
the miraculous works of these ancient folk. Their
beliefs and knowledge were passed on in fragmented
form to the Druids. Merlin was not a Druid, though
many thought him one. He, like Morgan Le Fey
and the other two ladies, was of a blood line that
still could be traced to the Mabden or elven folk.

At Arthur's court there was a great tolerance of
such people for the king owed his life and much
of his wisdom to Merlin. Many times Arthur had
been saved by both Merlin's magic and the weapons
given him by the Ladies of the Lake. Their prophecies
had also proven most beneficial. So we have it that
although Camelot was outwardly a devout Christian
community, it had its roots deep in the ways of a
race that was in its twilight age and spoke to gods
who were older than man.

Thus it was that even though Arthur knew his
sister to be treacherous, he still would not banish
her. Merlin had taught him many of the old ways

when he was but a lad, yet Arthur still could not fully grasp the reasoning of the elven folk. He had to be content to indulge them courteously and be on guard at all times.

Arthur knew, even before he had received Guinevere's message, that she would not join him in welcoming Morgan Le Fey to Camelot. There had been bad blood between these two ladies since the first day Guinevere had come to court. Lady Le Fey had openly told Arthur, and all others who were listening, that his new queen would never give him a son. This was enough to cause deep and grievous feelings between the women, but when the beautiful sorceress introduced Sir Modred at court as Arthur's bastard son and rightful heir to the throne, Guinevere's resentment flared into true hatred.

After reading Guinevere's terse note, Arthur instructed a page to guide Lady Le Fey to a small room off the main hall where he would receive her in privacy. He then stood for a time at a many-paned window watching his people in the snow bow to the mysterious queen as she entered the gates. He noticed his right hand had formed a fist which he quickly relaxed, and then he hurried to the small reception room. When she was shown into the room, Arthur nodded politely but neither spoke until they were left alone.

"Welcome, my sister," said Arthur with a faint smile. "What brings you to us on such a snowy day?"

"I come seeking your aid, dear brother," said the darkly handsome woman. "A fortnight has passed since my troubles first began."

"Pray continue," sighed Arthur.

She ignored his ill manners and said, "A monstrous beast now prowls the depth of Alder Wood.

This in itself would present no problem for few ever travel this gloomy land, but I do rely on what little game is to be found there to feed my people through the winter. My huntsmen now say there are no deer and even the hare have fled."

"I shall send you enough venison to last the winter," said Arthur amiably.

" 'Tis not this aid I seek, dear brother," she said irritably. "I care not for such charity. My purpose is to rid the forest of this foul beast. He has already killed several of my vassals."

"I see," said Arthur stroking his short golden beard. "You wish my men to go where yours have failed." Before she could retort, he continued. "Describe this beast, my sister."

Some of the anger left the lady's face as she said, " 'Twould best be likened to a horse, my lord, but hardly the likes of any you have seen. He is an enormous creature and, I fear, not of this world."

"Do not be certain that I have not viewed this very beast," said Arthur showing quick interest. "Is his coat the darkest of blacks?"

"Aye, my lord!" gasped Lady Le Fey. "He is the color of new pitch with eyes of fire!"

"He remains without a rider?" asked Arthur.

"None has been seen though he does carry a saddle and bridle. Who could ride such an animal?" she asked.

"One who calls himself Raum and professes to be a noble from a far-off land." The king quickly related to his sister the tragic events of Duncansby and the treachery of the mysterious knight called Raum. "He seems to be in league with the Viking horde but looks little like them. He stands over seven feet tall and is heavy with muscle. For his size he is uncommonly agile as many of our poor people have learned. His skin is a dark-olive color that has a strange coolness about it. His eyes are the same as those of his mount, fiery bright. His smile would make the bravest of men cold with loathing for it is crowned with two sharp fangs."

The dark queen paced in deep concentration as she listened to Arthur's description of the dreaded warrior. She stopped and gazed into the king's eyes as she said, "I'm sure that you've guessed this is no ordinary man, my brother. I'm sure also that you might think him some denizen of the netherworld called forth by myself."

"Such thoughts did come to mind," said Arthur calmly.

"Well, dispel any thought that the responsibility could be mine. I do agree, however, that we do face a being most formidable regardless from whence he comes. Does the presence of his mount signify he too lingers in Alder Wood? What purpose has he there?"

"Enough!" said the king loudly. "I have not such answers as yet but hopefully I soon shall. Reports have come to us that a young prince from farthest Finmark has come to Scotland seeking this very knight. He aided the King of Orkney in destroying the Norse fleet that had sacked Duncansby and Gavinshire. I have dispatched Lancelot to go forth and bring him here that we may learn more of this new enemy."

"When is Lancelot expected at court with the prince?"

"I would guess tomorrow. You are quite welcome to stay the night with us if you so choose."

"Indeed I shall, kind brother. I have need to
visit with Ladies Viviene and Nimue, with your
kind permission."

"By all means. I shall send word for them to
dine with you this evening in your quarters."

Lady Le Fey's eyes sparkled mischievously as she
said, "I had hoped to dine with you and your lovely
queen, my brother, but I do understand Guinevere
is feeling poorly. 'Tis nothing of a serious nature,
I'm sure . . . it seldom is with the queen."

Arthur strode from the room without reply.

When the three ladies sat before the fire in
Morgan Le Fey's quarters they seemed no different
than any of the other lovely women of Camelot;
but after a delicious dinner, that had been over-
seen personally by Lady Viviene, the servants cleared
the table and upon their departure the three ladies
leaned to conversation and it was then they seemed
changed.

"How has my brother received you here?" asked
Lady Le Fey of Viviene.

"Kindly, my lady," smiled the dark beauty. "I
was about to ask the same of you."

"He was civil," sniffed the sorceress queen airily.

Lady Nimue clucked her tongue at them and
said, "Be not unkind to dear Arthur. He has ever
been most kind and generous to all our elven folk.
He would never have scorned either of you had
you not committed mischiefs against him, his queen
and his knights."

"Do not be too pious, my sister," rejoined
Viviene. "Were it known to the king that 'twas you
who stole Merlin from him, I daresay you would not
enjoy his hospitality long."

"Little will be gained by womanly bickering," said Morgan Le Fey sternly. "It was agreed that our people needed someone at Arthur's court, Lady Nimue, and since your marriage to King Pelleas, who is beloved by the king and a devoted knight of the Round Table, it followed that 'twould be best that you undertake this task. We all three were in accord that if the king suspected you of doing away with the magician we would plant hints at court that in truth it was Viviene who was guilty and she would flee to our isle."

"Why must we live with this deception?" asked Nimue. "I am quite willing to risk the king's anger and confess my part in the disappearance and trust to his great sense of justice and mercy."

"Ha!" laughed Lady Le Fey. "You are such a child, Nimue! You must ask for either Arthur's mercy or his justice, you cannot have both for they are quite opposed to one another."

"I shall ask the king's understanding!" cried Nimue.

"You are the last of the elven folk that my brother still will trust!" shouted Morgan Le Fey. "If he finds he can no longer trust you he may well turn on us all. No Nimue, you shall not confess but continue as we have agreed for it is an unfortunate fact that we need Arthur far more than he needs us."

"Besides," laughed Viviene slyly, "there is already one at court that suspects me of the deed."

"Who would that be?" asked Nimue surprised.

"Percival," answered Viviene. "He cannot forgive me for the enchantment I placed upon his fellow knights turning them to stone. He near strangled me before I lifted the spell from them."

"Ah, that I could but recant the sorcery I did place upon Merlin," moaned Nimue, "but this secret was never revealed to me."

"Hush such talk!" ordered Lady Le Fey. "If the power to do so was ours, 'twould be only folly to do so. Merlin has long been the watchdog of Arthur and did prevent my acting upon the plans I have held so long."

"I have learned much from my brother this day," she replied, a smile playing at her scarlet lips. "I am now convinced that the beast of Alder Wood belongs to a knight not of this world."

"A demon?" cried Viviene gleefully.

"Indeed," replied the regal queen. "This creature, it seems, has killed many, and openly insulted the king. I know not where he now abides but I do hope he would return to recover his hellish mount. I would give much for an audience with him."

"For what purpose?" asked Nimue.

"I would like very much," said Lady Le Fey, to enlist his enmity of Arthur to my own design. With his strength and magical power the kingdom could be ours!"

"My lady!" whispered Nimue. "You speak too freely!"

"Have no fear," laughed the evil queen, "the king is too trusting to have spies within his own castle. But to my plan, fair sisters. Tomorrow Lancelot arrives with a young prince from the far north. This boy knows much of the demon we seek. Perhaps he will divulge how best we might entice the dreadful knight to our cause."

A banquet was prepared to welcome the foreign prince. He was presented to Arthur and Guinevere with much ceremony and pomp. After Prince Jal had been introduced by Lancelot to the lords and ladies, Arthur led the boy into the banquet hall where he seated him to his right with the queen to his left. As the company dined on the excellent food Arthur urged the young noble to relate his story which he readily did, much to the delight of the elven ladies who shared their table. The others were also delighted with the prince but sorrowed at his telling of the death of his father and the destruction of his kingdom at the hands of the demonic knight Raum.

"Do you think him dead?" asked Guinevere.

"I fear not, Your Highness," replied Jal. "There was no sign of him at Orkney and, I am told, a knight of your court did wound him south of here near Alder Wood."

"Tell me, brave prince," asked Morgan Le Fey, "since his charger still roams that forest do you think it possible this unholy knight might return there?"

"This news is most cheering to me, my lady," said the prince, "for I knew nothing of this. To answer your question I should say it is likely that Raum would return for his mount since few others would suit one of his size."

"But you are smiling, dear prince," purred Lady Viviene. "What good fortune or merriment do you find in such reports?"

"I have forsaken my mother, sweetheart and country that I may find and slay this demon-knight."

A murmur of surprise and awe went 'round the great dining table. Arthur placed a hand on the youth's shoulder saying, "Even at this court where bravery is a tradition your courage does inspire us, Prince Jal."

"Then I should confess, Your Majesty, that it is

not so much bravery that drives me as it is hatred," said the boy quietly.

"And if this hatred were to cease, good prince?" asked Gawain.

"You ask if I would be a coward, sir knight, and I take it you speak not to insult but out of honest interest. I shall say only that when first I met Raum in battle there was no hatred for him; yet 'twas I alone who wounded him that day."

"I bow to you, my prince, and pledge my service to your quest if my liege but release me from my duties here at Camelot," said Gawain.

"You shall not!" protested Lady Nimue. "The wounds from your first meeting with this knight have not yet healed."

"Verily a truth," said Guinevere. "Do not undo that which the good ladies have done with their nursing, lusty knight. 'Twould be only folly to send you against such an enemy when you are not yet fit."

"But I, my queen, am fit and quite eager to serve in Gawain's stead." All eyes turned to the youthful knight who spoke. He stood and bowed to Jal saying, "I am Sir Percival, my prince, and if the king permits it I shall join you in your quest. Also I would request my king release me from my former vows to not draw a blade against this evil knight."

"Both are granted," said Arthur.

Not far north of Alder Wood and a little way from the sea was the village of Wickscairn. The dwellings that formed the outer edge of this hamlet were, in truth, farms with lands stretching away from the village proper. One Jeremy of Wickscairn was the owner of one of these small farms, 'though a vassal to the king. He was a robust man in his middle years who lived alone due to his wife's death three years previous and no children from this most unsatisfactory marriage. It would be fair to say little if anything satisfied this man other than the acquiring of gold or a good warm flagon of ale. Compared to other small landholders, Jeremy fared far better than most for he did not have to provide for a growing family. Even his dealings at market, it was said, and his sharing with the king were overly shrewd if not dishonest. In brief, he was a wealthy man by the standards of that time, but not a well-thought-of man among his neighbors. Little wonder that the portly man had to seek his occasional female companionship from Nell, the openly shunned but privately courted harlot of Wickscairn.

It was a bright day with heavy snow on the thatch roofs of the buildings that formed Jeremy's farm. A pony cart made slow progress up the winding lane to the farm house. Jeremy stepped from his door to meet it puffing clouds of ale-scented breath into the frosty air. Nell sat in the cart wrapped in warm blankets, her nose a cherry-red. Jeremy took the reins from her without a greeting and led the pony to a low shed that housed hay from last summer's cutting. He swung the door wide and the cart was drawn into the dark interior.

"Gor! 'Tis black and musty in here," exclaimed Nell stepping from the cart as Jeremy tied the pony to a supporting timber.

"Ah yes, lass," said Jeremy smiling for the first time since her arrival, "but you can't deny it is warm."

"A good fire would be warmer, m'lord," retorted the plump girl. "Let's hurry to your house. I'm all anxious to see it, you know."

"Aye, that I do," he said not moving to leave the shed. "I have been thinking hard about your insisting that we meet here at my poor home instead of at your rooms as is customary. Methinks I know your purpose, naughty girl."

"What would you be saying?" cried Nell.

"You have too long listened to stories of my wealth and believing them did plan to tire me to sleep leaving you to take what e'er you desired."

"Here now!" protested the girl. "Is that any way to speak of a lady who holds you dear? My only plan was to have our time together more private and comfortable for you, wicked man."

"Well, here we have such privacy and warm hay does offer all the comfort that is needed."

"Here, m'lord? Well I never!"

"Yes you have, wench, so come here and give old Jeremy a kiss."

"Couldn't you close the door first? The wind that blows in is bitter."

With a shrug of his round shoulders he stalked to the door and shut it. The shed's interior was instantly plunged into inky blackness.

"Over here, love," called Nell. "Do be careful. Reach out your hand . . . Oh! You naughty thing!"

"I can't kiss you proper if you keep up your jabber, girl."

"You've never been given to the romantic, have you, love?" she complained.

"Why would I be romantic with the town slut?" he asked with a laugh.

There was silence for a moment until the pony cried out nervously, then Jeremy said in the darkness, "Ah, that's a good lass, Nell, hold me close and let

our nimble fingers do their duty with my buttons.
Vhat are you about? What . . . Nell!"

She shoved the thin blade deep into Jeremy's round
tomach and jumped quickly back, but he caught her
y the arm and pulled her with him as he fell into the
ay. She was pinned by the weight of the dying man.

"Why?" gasped Jeremy weakly.

"You were right, love," hissed Nell trying to
truggle free. "What I most want from you is in your
ouse and not your puny purse. I know you have
old a'plenty that even the king has not been made
ware of. I'm sick of being pawed and handled by the
ikes o'you. No more of your bad manners and
buses, Jeremy. Now die like the gentleman you
ever were!"

His hand was at her throat but without the
trength to close. He breathed his last in a little
urgle of bloody spittle.

After working herself free of the weight of the
orpse, Nell felt her way through the darkness to the
loor which she opened slightly to permit a little light
nto the barn. The pony was now whinnying shrilly and
tamping about in the hay. Jeremy's inert figure could
arely be seen in the dim light. She went to it and
ulled the dagger free wiping it on the man's coat.
he slipped the blade into the folds of her clothing
nd went to where the horse was tied. She had just
ouched the knot when a shadow crossed the light
rom the slightly ajar door. Whirling she saw, much
o her horror, the silhouette of a monstrous figure
laring at her with eyes of fire.

"God protect me!" screamed Nell.

Rumbling laughter came from the dark figure be-
ore it said, "You pray well for one who whores,
teals and has just now murdered."

"Who are you?" she cried, fumbling for the knife in her skirts.

"Your dearest friend," laughed the sinister intruder.

"How are you my friend?"

"I choose not to kill you, my bloody girl, at least for the present. That should make me a very dear friend indeed."

"What . . . what will you do with me?"

"I should like you to give me simple instruction on how I might go to Dolorous Garde, home of the fabled sorceress Morgan Le Fey."

"I knew it!" cried the girl. "You are the devil himself come to bed that evil queen!"

"Your speculations are amusing but not informative, dear girl. Now tell me what I must know else I shall twist your babbling head from your ample body." He suddenly was upon her catching her arm before she could drive the blade home. She screamed in agony as he crushed her soft wrist causing the dagger to fall to the hay-strewn floor. The terrifying giant threw her into a corner by some sacks of seed as though she were a discarded doll. He loomed above her and shouted, "Now tell me the way to the castle!"

"South!" cried the hysterical girl. "Go south to the well at the crossroad and turn to your left. That road is little used except by those going to Dolorous Garde. This way takes you through a part of Alder Wood to the marshes. 'Tis here you'll find the castle rising out of the water, a long causeway joining it to the land."

"Very good, sweet girl," chuckled the dark figure. "Is there anything else I should be told?"

"You must take care, m'lord," said Nell in a somewhat calmer voice. "A beast now roams that rest and kills without reason. A monstrous horse it black as night and eyes . . ." Her voice died with a whimper.

"Like mine, sweet Nell?" laughed the menacing shadow. She began to cry in a pitiful way which only made him laugh louder. "You know," he said, "you and your fat friend disturbed my sleep today here in his shed. I have traveled most of the night and need rest. This does pose a problem doesn't it, Nell? I cannot go back to sleep and have you fleeing to the king's men to blame me for the carving up of poor Jeremy, now can I? There are other reasons too that the king should not know my whereabouts. No, I would never travel the road in this light nor can I risk letting you go. It does seem we must enjoy each other's company for the day. Now make a place in the hay there for us to be . . . comfortable."

He reached down and tore her shirtfront downward exposing her large breasts to the dim light. "Oh please, my lord!" begged Nell.

"Of course," he said quietly, "I could strangle you now with your pretty hair."

"Oh, my lord, do leave and spare me!" she moaned. "I swear I shall tell no one of our meeting."

He leaned and gathered her in his great arms. "If you treat me well this day, wicked lass, you might live to see tomorrow's sun, though I feel sparing you would be a risk I can ill afford."

When her screams increased only the gathered ravens were there to hear.

For three days and nights the ladies sat in the sacred circle and chanted their incantations.

"Tarvis glon, nemi tarvis, aroon, aroon, aroon," intoned Morgan Le Fey.

"Coomb aroon," whispered Lady Viviene a
Lady Nimue.

The vapors from the ceremonial pot at the cent
of the circle had remained a dull blue these pa
days but well into the third night the smoky bl
turned a radiant green. Lady Le Fey's dark ey
danced as she watched the cloud of vapor rise abo
them. The other ladies smiled and continued the
chants. A dark shadow seemed to undulate with
the cloud.

" 'Tis the beast of the wood!" said Viviene starin
upward.

"Yet now he has his rider," purred Lady Le Fey.

"My lady, he comes!" gasped Lady Nimue.

"He sees that dawn is near," said the hig
sorceress. "He will not approach this castle wi
light. He knows we wait for him but he is wary. I
trusts no one." She passed her hand through th
vapor and the vision quickly faded. Turning to th
other two ladies she said, "After the sun has rise
Lady Nimue, I shall wake Sir Percival and request h
see you safely back to Camelot. I want no you
gallant interfering with our plans now."

"But he does seem intent in his search for th
beast, Morgana," said Nimue using Lady Le Fey
more intimate name to indicate she was not objectin
to the queen's proposal, only pointing to an are
that could become a problem.

"But Percival knows nothing of the evil knight
arrival. To him the beast is still alone in the fores
Let it remain so. I shall stress the importance of you
return to Camelot. His devotion to his fellow knigh
and their good health will prevail. Now do get you
things ready for travel. The sky grows bright in th
east."

Sir Percival refused the company of any of organ Le Fey's guardsmen in his escorting of ady Nimüe to Camelot. He loathed these foul men--arms and would have no more to do with them an duty demanded. He and Lady Nimüe made eedy progress riding their fine mounts upon the inding road through Alder Wood. At one place in e brooding forest the young knight noticed an ncommon number of ravens soaring above the ngled treetops. He immediately recalled such birds Duncansby and he believed he had heard their lls the night the fire in the forest had nearly aimed Gawain. He wondered at this sign and was uch tempted to plunge into the wintry wood to see the infernal knight hid there. Upon consideration owever, he knew he could not involve Lady Nimüe nd her safety in such an adventure. Their horses ced on and soon they had left the wood and passed e well at the crossing.

When they entered the lane through Wickscairn, ey were hailed by a white-haired man waving his rms. There were others close behind him as Percival nd the lady reined in their horses.

"What ho, my good man?" asked the youthful night. "Can I or my king be of service here?"

"In truth you can, my lord," said the man. "A rrible deed has been done here and we must get ord to the sheriff or the king this day."

"How so?" asked Percival.

"Murder, your lordship," cried the man. "A fine llow from our village was slain and a wench near ain."

"Who did this thing?"

"The lass tells it badly as you might well under-tand for she suffered greatly, but her story is a

strange one. She says a dark giant with eyes of fir
did kill poor Jeremy and forced himself upon h
sweet body."

"The fiend!" cursed Percival, his hand goir
instinctively to his sword. "Where may I find th
poor maid and speak with her?"

"She be with the ladies at chapel, my lord."

Percival and Nimue rode to the little village churc
and arrived as a group of women emerged leadin
the ravaged girl. The lady who seemed most i
command of the proceedings was a large shapeles
mound of clothing topped with a long pointy nos
and bright ferret eyes. This was the widow Wiggir
whose voice carried much influence in the affairs c
Wickscairn. The young knight addressed himself t
this imposing dame.

"Greetings, sad ladies, from Arthur, king of all th
Britons, myself Sir Percival, knight of the Roun
Table and Lady Nimue, wife and queen to Kin
Pelleas who stands in great honor at Camelot."

"Praise be to you and the lady," replied Widov
Wiggins. "Your arrival is most timely, sir knight. Her
stands the outraged maiden Nell, her wits still nc
settled from her hellish experience. 'Tis justice sh
seeks, gallant knight, and 'tis justice we demand."

"The king's justice shall prevail, good woman," sai
Percival with resolution. He stepped down from hi
mount and went to the sniffling Nell. "Tell me of th
crime, sad child," he invited.

"Dare not ask me, gentle knight," cried Nell, "bu
since you must, I must needs to answer you. 'Twa
three days ago that sweet Jeremy had me to his farn
to propose marriage to me. Oh, that poor sweet man!"
she sobbed. "Few really knew my Jeremy. Most sav
him as a widowed pinchpenny, but not so. Generou

nd sweet he was, so much so that since he had ex-
erienced the loss of his dear wife three years past,
e grew to have great concern for the poor ladies of
ur village that had suffered a like loss and had no
ne to care for them. That very day . . . that day
hat shall always bring horror and grief to my poor
eart . . . sweet Jeremy did ask me for my hand
aying that 'twas a pity that he should fall in love
vith me for it was the widow ladies he did feel great
orrow for and would like to help and give them a
ood home with lands and what security such things
ring."

"Truly a great man has died here!" cried Percival
viping Nell's tears with his glove.

"Your perception and kindness is a credit to the
ing's court," said Widow Wiggins.

"Do go on," urged Lady Nimue remaining calm
nd indifferent to the high emotions of the rest.

"Well, since I must, though it pains me greatly,"
vhimpered Nell, "I quickly praised dear Jeremy for
his sympathy to the unfortunate ladies of the vil-
age. He seemed glad that I understood and asked a
vow from me that after we had wed . . . if anything
vere to . . . if he should pass away to his heavenly
eward, I should live in comfort and not be lonely."

"You are the very angel of charity," gasped
Percival kissing Nell's hand.

"But they did not wed," reminded Nimue.

"Alas, that is the rub," said Widow Wiggins. "We
seek your help, good sir, in carrying out this fine man's
ast wishes."

"How may I help?" asked the young knight
eagerly.

"You must go to our generous king and ask him to
rule that Jeremy's lands go to sweet Nell so that the

love and charity of this sainted man live on here
Wickscairn."

"A noble monument to a noble man," agree
Percival. "I will ride quickly to Camelot and retur
with his answer before the week is past. Farewel
saddened ladies."

"Hold, Sir Percival!" cried Lady Nimue. "Are w
not forgetting our main concern?"

"How so, my lady?" asked the knight mountin
his horse. "One of the great laws of chivalry is t
aid and serve ladies in distress."

"But what of the crime?" exclaimed Nimue.

"Oh yes, that," said Widow Wiggins with a grea
sigh. "A brute attacked them in the barn where the
were putting Nell's horse away. He split Jeremy's b
belly with his dirk and did set about raping poor Nel
Let us talk no more of this as it does upset the swee
girl."

"But what of the murderer?" asked Nimue.

"From the man's description when we entered th
village," said Percival airily, "I would guess it to b
Raum. Since no one here is fleeing for their lives,
would also guess him gone from here. Now be kin
Lady Nimue, and press the lass no further."

"You are the prince of all knights!" gushed Nel
kissing his foot where it hung in its stirrup.

"Perhaps the wretched girl wishes you to stay th
night," commented Nimue sourly.

"Mercy no!" exclaimed Widow Wiggins as sh
pulled Nell away from Percival's charger. " 'Tis bes
you see the king about our problems as soon as i
possible, sweet knight. Your staying here throug
the night would only expose your gentle innocence t
a very shabby trait of our otherwise good townfolk.

"What trait is this?" asked Percival.

"We are given to much unfounded gossip, if you will, kind sir," explained the widow, "and I must confess I am as guilty as any of this terrible habit. There have been times I might have said unkind things even about poor Nell here. Now this awful tragedy has shown us her true heart so I say ride quickly, noble knight, on your mission of mercy and listen not to the likes of us."

"I judge this good advice, my lord," smiled Nimue.

"It takes a great lady to admit her errors, dear widow," said Percival, "and may the Lord protect you until my return."

The ladies waved their goodbys as the knight and lady rode from the village toward Camelot.

Under a moonless sky and once more upon the back of his black charger, the towering warrior came to the gates of Dolorous Garde. Though his cloak was the color of night his arrival did not go undetected. Somewhere in the darkness a raven cried out a warning causing the shadowed giant's helmeted head to turn suddenly. Flaming red eyes gazed down at the water's edge where a figure crept forward, ax in hand. The stalker's arm quickly arched and sent the heavy blade flying. It flashed by the knight's head and lodged in the heavy timbers of the gate.

A second later the quiet was shattered by the man's screams as the knight's dark lance skewered him and lifted him high like a wiggling sausage. A torch appeared on the wall above the gate. The newcomer with the light cried out when the impaled guard appeared out of the dark space before him. The guard was now dead, eyes staring as if they were made of glass, blood and bile pouring freely from his open mouth. When the giant's fist struck the gate a terrible blow, the poor fellow on the wall dropped his brand and ran screaming from sight.

Silence followed for a time and then heavy timbers were drawn from inside the gate letting the doors swing open. Hand-held fires revealed heavily armed men within and in their midst stood the darkly beautiful Queen of Dolorous Garde. The menacing knight urged his great mount forward into the courtyard. He lowered his lance to the queen and in turn dropped the body of the unfortunate vassal at her feet.

"I do hope my attracting spell has not inconvenienced you, Lord Raum," said Morgan Le Fey ignoring the corpse lying before her.

If he was surprised at her knowing his identity he did not show it. "Not at all, my lady, for your magic can take little credit for my coming. My destination has been this castle for some time now."

A startled look flickered in the queen's dark eyes, for an unguarded moment, then quickly she said, "And why should one of your rank come all the way from Netherworld, unbidden, to this humble court?" She had a nervous little laugh as she added, "Who has sent you to end my poor life?"

"I come freely of my own will," laughed Raum. "I come not to harm any, my lady, but I will tolerate no interference so be warned."

"None here wishes to conflict with your plans, dreaded knight, for we too have plans, the which we would discuss with you. Perhaps the two would go together well."

"Do you offer hospitality, dark lady?"

"Indeed!" smiled Lady Le Fey holding a slender white hand out to him. "My castle is your home so long as you like, my lord. Come, let us leave this cold night air and sup by a warm fire. You may then tell me the true nature of your visit."

As an act of goodwill, Lady Le Fey dismissed her guards and all left with the exception of one big fellow who remained at her side. His piggish eyes never left off watching the demon-knight but Raum seemed to pay him no notice.

"Do quit your great steed," instructed the queen, "and put him in yonder stable where there is feed and warmth for him."

"You are too gracious, my lady," said Raum matching her smile as he dismounted and did as she had said. He then followed her down a dimly lit passage to the castle's great hall.

Few windows graced the big room and these were very high, lost in the gloom among the blackened beams overhead. An enormous fireplace stood at the end of the room, the fire sending shadows from its blackened maw like phantoms leaping across the stone walls. Upon these walls hung tapestries depicting men, women, animals and monsters in various erotic and cruel games. Grotesque statuary leered from every corner and recess. Raum sensed that beyond the circle of firelight slithered unnameable things of the dark.

A great deal of hot food was upon the table indicating that the queen had indeed been expecting a guest. Raum took the seat she offered and immediately set to eating the food before him. He never spoke nor looked at either the queen or her guard until he felt he had at last had his fill.

"Was the meal to your liking, my lord?" asked the queen.

"Aye, that it was," replied Raum wiping his mouth

with the back of his hand, "but perhaps a little more poison would have increased my pleasure."

Once more fear leaped to her eyes. "My lord! What can you mean by such words?"

"Do relax, lovely lady," he said with a crooked grin. " 'Twas only a feeble jest. You are overly defensive."

Seeing that Raum made no threat to the lady nor her brutish guard they did relax. "A habit," she said with her warm smile, "one that I shall try to overcome while in your presence, my lord, for I am frequently falsely accused."

Raum laughed showing his unusual teeth as he said, "Take care with your words, dark lady, when speaking to me for I have served the king of liars."

She joined him in his laughter then and said, "If your lordship would like a glass of wine, I promise to use a bit more poison."

His laughter now shook the great hall causing the obscene hangings to shift as in a slight breeze. The queen poured the wine into heavy goblets of purest gold. She sprinkled a blue-green powder over the surface of the drink she handed him.

"This," she said, "should kill the stink of your mighty breath and make our talk more pleasing for me. If you are to speak with mortals, Lord Raum, you must have done with the smell of hell about your breath."

"I do hope your powder's effect is long lasting," he laughed, "as I shall be among men for some time, dear lady."

"My potion should last forever and a day," she laughed merrily, "but do tell me of your reasons for seeking me out."

"Without delay," agreed the awesome knight emptying his cup with a noisy gulp. "I come to you for aid." His eyes flickered as he became aware that someone stood nearby in the shadows. He sensed it was a woman and that she offered no threat to him.

"How could I possibly help one of your great power?" asked Morgan Le Fey.

"I seek the magician Merlin. I am told by others that 'tis you who holds knowledge of his whereabouts. I have sought after him among the souls of the newly dead to no avail."

"Ah, but you have been told the whole truth, my gallant knight. You must reveal your need for Merlin if I am to tell you where he is."

The smile left Raum's evil features. His hand quickly shot forward and grabbed a great fistful of her hair. "You mistake my meaning. I came not to bargain!" he said through bared teeth.

The guard leaped to his feet, sword in hand, but a moment later the blade clattered to the floor from his trembling fingers as his head was caught and held in the tightening grip of Raum's huge hand. The man's screams continued even after a large thumb had entered one of his eye sockets and probed bloodily toward his terror-stricken brain.

The queen stared, fascinated, as Raum's grip increased on the weakening skull. A dull cracking sound was heard and the man's cries ceased, his head now a jellied pulp in the monstrous knight's hand.

"Too fast, my lord!" came a soft feminine voice from the shadows. Raum turned and watched her step into the light. Viviene's gown was a flowing silk in shades of deepest blue. Her green eyes were wide with wonder and lust. Her beautiful ruby lips parted in a childlike smile. "You did it much too fast," she breathed.

Raum's angry eyes shifted from the ecstatic girl to Morgan Le Fey whose hair he still held tightly. He pulled the queen's head into his lap where he twisted her dark locks so that the skin of her lovely face was stretched to near tearing. He seemed deaf to all her pleas.

Lady Viviene came to his side and watched in mute fascination as he put forth a bloody finger and plucked a tiny ant from the floor. So tight was the flesh of the queen's fine features that she found closing her eyes to be quite impossible. Raum gently dropped the insect onto one of her exposed eyes and smiled, as did Viviene, while Lady Le Fey screamed her sanity away.

At last he released her dark tresses and the ant was washed away in a flood of tears. Raum looked about at the gathering of men who had been summoned by the queen's loud cries. All had weapons drawn but stood their ground out of fear that a charge would mean their queen's life. Raum showed them a mirthless smile as he spoke a strange word that none recognized. Tiny flame serpents slid from the great hearth and approached the terrorized men-at-arms.

"Leave us now," demanded Raum of the guards, "or watch your mistress die a hideous death." The fire-serpents hissed loudly and the men broke into open panic scrambling through the doorways to escape. The knight spoke once more and the serpents slithered across the stones to the hearth and vanished as they had come.

"Now, my lady," he said turning his attention to the queen, "you shall answer all questions I put to you."

"At your pleasure," sobbed the defeated lady.

"What have you done with the magician?"

"He lies entombed beneath the earth till the end of

all days," she moaned, "but 'twas not my doing, foul knight."

Raum noticed the other lady shrink back toward the shadows now. He pointed a finger at her and commanded, "Stay you there!" She stopped but said nothing.

Morgan Le Fey's look of fear quickly changed to one of anger as she pointed to Viviene and said, "There is your answer, Lord Raum. There is the lady who seduced Merlin's magic from him and turned it upon the old magician sealing him beneath a great stone."

"You seem not to lie, wise lady," smiled Raum to the disheveled sorceress. "Who is your lovely and blood-thirsty friend?"

"She's my handmaid and pupil Lady Viviene."

"Come here, lass," ordered Raum motioning to Viviene.

"Fear not, sweet and mischievous child," said the queen. "Lord Raum will do us no harm if you tell what he wishes to hear."

"My lady!" cried Viviene. "I implore you not to set this cruel and marvelous knight upon me, for the deed that concerns him I did not do!" The girl with the silky black hair now threw herself at Raum's feet speaking in a frightened voice. "Her lie has fooled even you, my lord."

Raum glanced sharply at Lady Le Fey and then struck her with his open hand sending her crashing to the floor. He stood over the cowering woman shouting, "You did trick me, queen of vipers. Since it was another who done the deed, I took the rest of what you said to be true. I see my error now just as I see that this girl at my feet is not guilty. Since you chose to accuse her falsely I now give her the privilege of selecting the fashion of your death."

"My lord, no!" shrieked the queen. "It is true I did avoid the whole truth but for a reason. 'Twas a sacred agreement between three ladies of the old ways. We vowed none should tell that it was the third lady who sealed Merlin in his cave. She is too valuable to our people in her position at Arthur's court."

"I care nothing for your cat-and-mouse intrigues," said Raum. "Tell me that which I ask or you shall surely die this night."

"You have the truth, my lord," said Viviene, her voice becoming somewhat calmer now. She stood up and looked full into his blazing eyes. "We cannot give the name of our elven sister but that does not prevent us from aiding you in your quest to reach the magician."

"Are you saying the spell that imprisons Merlin can be broken?" asked Raum beginning his evil smile.

"You, my lord, know that any spell can be broken if there is enough will in the breaking."

"Very good, my lovely," said Raum running a hand down her slender back. "You have taught this girl well, Lady Le Fey."

"She surpasses even me, my lord. She conjures demons and spirits of the dead to teach her now," said Morgan Le Fey.

He put both of his broad hands on her shoulders and instead of pulling away she proudly thrust her firm breasts forward. He released her and asked, "Do you know the whereabouts of Merlin's confinement?"

"Aye, my lord," she said, "I have projected to it many times but the curse that seals it is a powerful one. My inner sight and mind are unable to penetrate its great force. But you have a will superior, I should guess, to that of any mortal."

"Very well," said the demon-knight. "I shall go to my quarters and rest through the coming day. When night comes next we shall begin the attempt to penetrate the cave."

"Show his lordship to his room, Viviene," said the queen, "then return here to me."

"She will stay with me," stated Raum. Viviene's green eyes widened in surprise for a moment before she stepped to Raum's side and smiled self-consciously at the furious queen.

Viviene brought feelings to Raum that were totally alien to him. By the dim light he studied her perfect features as she lay sleeping in his arms. She seemed childlike, yet even before they had made love he knew this woman could master any man if she truly desired it. The gentleness that sprang from her woman's breast could change in an instant to an evil violence that shook even this monstrous knight. All in all she seemed a glorious savage who reveled in sensual delights and the suffering of others. Raum's big hand stroked her black tresses as his mind was assaulted by questions and feelings of joy, fear and, at last he had to say the word, love.

Heavy drapes covered the window but enough light filtered about their edges to tell Raum that it was not yet evening. His mind was far too active for sleep so he quietly rose from the big bed and stared down at this evil, wanton girl who had now become so precious to him. As he leaned to brush her smooth cheek with a kiss he covered her flawless body with a heavy blanket of furs that had slipped from the bed. Her mouth turned up in a little smile as she murmured his name in her sleep.

He lifted a woolen blanket from a chair and wrapped it about his shoulders to stave off the cold that had settled upon the room since the fire on the hearth had died to a few glowing coals. As he placed new wood over the embers, a light tapping sounded at the room's heavy door. He quickly went across the room and opened it to find Morgan Le Fey standing before him with a tray of hot food and a cheery smile.

"I felt you were awake and knew you would be famished," she said.

Raum held up a finger to warn Lady Le Fey that Viviene still slept and that they should be quiet. She set the tray on a small table by the fire that was now blazing with new life.

"What now, Lord Raum?" asked the queen diverting her eyes from his gapping blanket. "You must be anxious to leave us and go to old Merlin."

"Ah, that it were so, my lady, for now I think only of remaining here in that sweet girl's arms."

"How ridiculous you seem this morning, hellish knight," mocked the queen. "You act like a love-sick youth! I was told that one of your kind is not given to such sweet and sickening feelings."

"Lovers always appear a little foolish to the world, Morgana," he replied affectionately, "yet few mock such behavior. Can you not recall being in love? Lovers want only that the world be as happy as they. Why do you not put aside your bad feelings and join us in our happiness?"

"You do make me ill, Lord Raum" she said as she poured them each a cup of steaming broth. "If your eyes were as clear as mine, you would see that Viviene could never love one such as you. Look at your appearance. Your body is huge . . . all of it. Yours is the face of hate and cruelty itself. In a word, Raum, you are ugly!"

"You are wrong!" came a cry from the bed. Viviene rose up out of the furs and glared at the queen. She threw the heavy covers aside and stepped into the firelight. Her white form was exquisite. Her black hair, like Raum's companions the ravens, showed blue highlights in the dim illumination. She moved to his side putting her arm about his waist. "Raum is the most beautiful creature in this world, my lady, and I feel you know this and are quite jealous."

Anger welled in the queen's eyes but she made no reply.

Raum smiled and pulled Viviene close saying, "You are right, my queen, I am ugly to some but Viviene sees me with love's eyes."

"As she does all men!" spat Lady Le Fey.

"Morgana!" cried Viviene. "Do not hold such hateful feelings for me. 'Tis not that I have turned against you. Your plan was to enlist this magical knight to our cause. 'Twould not further our cause to make him our enemy."

"Do you say you share his bed only to serve the elven folk? Liar!" shouted the queen. "The cloak of nobility is not yours to wear, Viviene."

"Silence!" ordered Raum. Gazing down at Viviene, he asked, "To enlist me to your purpose, was that your only motive?"

"At first it was, my gallant," said the young sorceress.

"And now?" he demanded.

"Have no fear, my knight of knights, I do love you as no other."

The brooding queen turned away as they kissed. She

stood glaring into the fire while they dressed. At last the vexed lady calmed enough to join them at their meal and sip her cup of broth. "You are right, my evil child," she said to Viviene, "we must put our different feelings aside and act as one if our plan is to succeed."

"Although I have feelings for Raum that are new and wonderful to my experience, dear lady," said Viviene, "if his company in your own bed would bring harmony between us, I would ask him to comply with your wishes."

The queen suddenly broke into laughter hugging Viviene as she said, "You are such a wicked child! 'Tis not that sort of companionship I seek. My fear was that I had lost your loyalty and friendship, lusty girl, and hearing that I have not I would suggest we turn our attention to Raum's quest for Merlin."

After the circle had been drawn, the fires lit and the strange symbols inscribed within its arc, Morgan Le Fey intoned a chant that soon brought a response from distant Lady Nimue.

"Yes, my lady," came Nimue's voice from the darkness above the heads of the two elven ladies and Raum.

"Do lend your life force to our cause this night, Nimue," said the queen. The fiery little pots about the circle hissed as she threw some powder into each. Turning to Raum she said, "We are ready, my lord."

Raum walked to where the circle was drawn upon the stone floor and after kneeling intoned another chant. He then lay prone before them, eyes closed and breathing heavily.

When the blue green mist drifted away from Raum's consciousness, he saw the magician prone among his books, jars and chests. He rested upon a pallet of skins near the back wall of the cave. An eerie radiance shone from huge jewels embedded in the stony walls. Raum felt a weakness in his legs and sat down upon one of the large chests. It was true; the curse upon Merlin's cave was a formidable one indeed. It had taken all the will he could muster and the aid from the three ladies for him to gain entry into the tomb. He gazed at the still form before him. There were no signs of life yet Raum did not despair. He placed a finger upon the aged forehead and spoke his strange words. Color began to show in Merlin's sunken cheeks. The old man's chest began a slow but perceptible rising and falling. At last the wrinkled eyelids fluttered under the bushy, white brows.

"Aah!" groaned Merlin. "Who wakes me from my blessed sleep that I so richly deserve?"

"Raum, Earl of Netherworld."

Merlin's pale eyes focused on the warrior's brutal features. "Hmm," mused the magician, "I recall nothing of dying and the spell was a most trusted enchantment. I must assume, my large friend, that this is in truth my cave and you are a trespasser. How is it you come to me unbidden?"

"No longer do I reside in Netherworld, old one. The world of the Mabden has become my home."

"I would imagine those you have met could hardly contain their joy at this news," groaned Merlin sitting up and scratching about his person. "Man is not ready for the likes of you nor, I dare say, are you ready for the world of man."

"Aye, that is so," smiled Raum.

"I shall not ask how you gained entry into my sacred cave," said Merlin attempting to stand but falling back among his blankets, "still I shall ask you why."

"I am driven to questioning," said Raum assisting the

magician to his feet. "I feel you are singularly qualified to answer some of these questions."

Merlin walked on wobbly legs to the hearth where he touched a blackened rock with his toe. It immediately burst into flame causing the wizard to jump away cursing his scorched toes. Recovering, he dipped some water into a kettle from a little stream in the rock and added some herb. After setting the kettle on the fire he turned to Raum and said, "I can hardly guess what answers I possess that you do not, Lord Raum."

"I have long held," said the warrior, "there is much that has been withheld from us of Netherworld by our Lord Lucifer."

"A reasonable assumption," commented Merlin as he worked at slicing some cheese and hard bread.

"Why would this be so?" asked Raum.

"Because if 'twere known by the lesser demons, such as yourself, my lord, that their cause was lost from the beginning, all would rebel against Lucifer's authority. 'Twould be hell for sure," cackled Merlin merrily. "You must understand, my lord, it was ordained from the first that although you, like man, should have free will to choose, we would all eventually choose that which is most compatible to us. It is a certainty that man and demon alike shall choose that from which he springs."

"Although I understand little of what you say," said Raum seating himself in a large chair at the magician's table, "your words seem to ring true to me. I have felt for some time that I must leave Netherworld and seek my true place."

Merlin still laughed as he placed the cheese before Raum. "You have only recognized what all men feel. Each senses deep within his own breast that he must struggle to excel and attain a place far above his present level of being. Yet few have come to recognize this as you have. It is that which one day man shall term evolutionary."

"Then I have been correct in my feelings?"

"Of course, poor wretch, but that is not to say your goal and task is a simple one. If I did not know the laws that be I would say your quest is an impossible one."

"But it is not? There are those who do achieve this goal?"

"To be sure," smiled Merlin lifting the pot from the fire and pouring its contents into two stone cups. "Young Gallahad has already reached this goal as will Sir Percival."

"Those two!" exclaimed Raum. "I knew them to be somehow different! Please tell me, good Merlin, why have I been unable to kill these knights . . . yea, even strike them?"

" 'Tis simple. The spark that dwells within you, and has from the beginning, recognizes the same in these two for they have near become that spark itself. So dear is your goal to you that you cannot deny it to those who are near to reaching it. Deep within you, deeper even than you have knowledge of, Lord Raum, there is an understanding that if even two reach this goal, your chances of achieving it are somehow improved. 'Tis a profound mystery."

"I do not pretend to understand, great Merlin," spoke Raum with humility, a trait he had never noticed in himself before, "but I shall do whatever you dictate to achieve this end. Although I detest him I would even follow in Percival's steps and be squire to him if he would not slay me first."

"Lord Raum, you speak with an idiot's tongue!" exclaimed Merlin. "If you permit Percival to slay you while you strive toward your highest goal, he is retarded in reaching that state himself and the curse will be on you both."

"Was this the thing that prevented my killing a bothersome priest recently?"

"Indeed. It is that deep knowledge I spoke of. Ah, sad knight, I must tell you also that you may not follow in young Percival's steps."

"How so?"

"He is innocent and you are not. You must surely die and reincarnate as a child, several times I fear, to finally be as innocent as he. Death is a purifier, my lord, in your case. With all your evil ways it would be a mammoth undertaking to achieve your high state while still possessing full knowledge of your evil experience."

"But I have no choice!" shouted Raum in frustration. "I cannnot die for if I should, my Lord Asteroth and Lucifer would hold and punish me forever in Netherworld. Whether it be to my liking or not, old one, I am destined to pursue a goal that is as elusive as quicksilver, and one that I myself do not understand, while not having the benefit of death."

"Ah," breathed Merlin shaking his head sadly and sipping the hot brew from his cup, "I have not thought of pitying one of your kind before but I do now. You see, my lord, Percival has a childlike innocence that enables him to reject this world and move to the next and higher realm. He is even a virgin. You do see the difficulty that lies ahead for you, do you not, my most unfortunate knight? It might take centuries to free yourself of this plane of existence just as it did for you to decide to escape your old regions."

"If not Percival, then who shall guide me?" moaned the dark giant.

"What has led you here?"

"This inner knowledge," replied Raum, "but it speaks seldom and not clearly."

"Aye, and your mistakes will be great and many, my lord, but this is the way you must go. God help mankind! Much blood shall be shed and great shall be the tragedy left in your wake," cried Merlin dusting crumbs of bread and cheese from his long, white beard.

"If this be wrong then I shall change," said Raum.

"You cannot change so simply," said Merlin. "You must grow to such changes. You must be true to your nature and as it changes so shall you. You will not reach your goal by lying to yourself, my lord."

"Then so be it!" shouted the warrior as he slammed his fist to the table with such force that it split in two, spilling food and drink onto the cavern floor. Neither the demon-knight nor the magician seemed aware of this destruction.

Merlin went to Raum and hugged him as he would a son and then went to his pallet.

"You choose to stay here in your confinement?" asked Raum. " 'Twould be no difficult task to shake the earth and break the stone that seals this place now that I am inside the enchantment."

"Put away your spell-breaking plans, my troubled friend," said Merlin setting himself among his blankets. "I sleep here in dreamless rest by choice. Why should I return to my lad Arthur who is now king and aid in his every judgment? He has relied on my powers far too long as it is. He is either a king or he is not. I know his end will come in a few short years and that this is ordained by a plan so high that it passes understanding. Yet I care not to stand by and watch these coming events which I cannot alter for I do love this lad who was once as a son to me.

"And why," continued the old magician now lying with eyes closed, "should I continue in a life where heavenly Nimue loves another? Do tell that fair thing that she should feel no blame for my absence. I did make a total pest of myself with her and did attempt to seduce her in this very cavern. She did only that which a lady should do. Tell her that I choose to stay here until that time when the earth shall be transformed into a higher order since I cannot have her."

"But you can put a spell on her!" blurted Raum. "I shall fetch her for you."

"There is no place for force in matters of love as you shall learn, my lord. Now, if you are done with your questions, I bid you farewell until we meet at the end of all days."

Upon his return to Wickscairn, Sir Percival extended the king's greeting and goodwill to the village leaders and gave full title to Jeremy's properties to Nell who in turn doled out much of it to the town widows. It was during this business that Nell happened to mention that the brute who had taken damnable liberties with her person had also asked the way to Dolorous Garde. This piece of information put Percival in a high state of excitement. Bidding the grateful Nell farewell, he left her, much to her dismay since her plans for him were otherwise. They stood in the lane cheering and waving to him as he rode quickly from the village toward Alder Wood.

The sorceress queen tapped lightly at the door before entering. Viviene stood across the room gazing out the window.

"Has Raum returned from his morning ride in the forest?" asked Lady Le Fey.

"Just now, my lady," replied the lovely temptress. "He is putting his horse away in the stable."

"I have come to ask you if you and your knight would breakfast with me this morning?"

" 'Twould be a pleasure to us both, Morgana," replied the girl.

The queen led the way and the two ladies had just entered the small dining room off to one side of the castle kitchen when a servant stepped through another door leading Raum. He bowed to the queen and kissed Viviene.

"How went your ride this morning?" asked Morgan.

"Very well, my lady," replied Raum smiling. He then turned to Viviene and said, "I named the horse as you instructed, my girl."

"What name did you choose?" asked the queen.

"He shall be called Eligor after a friend in Netherworld, a great knight who knows how to cause and fight a fine war."

"What sweet sentiment!" laughed Morgan and they joined her in her laughter. As they ate their meal they talked of things not serious until the queen said, "You tarry here, my lord, for many days now and you are welcome but I do remind you both that our plans for unseating Arthur from his throne must not be forgotten. I am cheered to see you happy in the company of one another whiling away the hours together, but there is work to be done."

"I want not to seem ungrateful, dear lady," said Raum, "yet I have no place in your plans. I have seen into the future of your adventure and know it will succeed without my assistance. By your woman's power you shall surely bring down noble Arthur."

"And what else do you see?" asked Morgan with growing interest.

"I see you and Lady Nimue with the dear king's corpse. You are in a boat returning from France."

"Then I shall win and Modred shall rule!" cried the queen.

"Not so, my lady," said Raum, "for the one you would have as king shall never be."

Morgan frowned and puzzled over the mystery of the knight's words.

"And what of me?" asked Viviene. "Did you not see me in your visions, my love?"

Raum remained silent.

Upon seeing the knight's hand tighten on his goblet Viviene asked, "What is it, my lord? Do tell me!"

"I saw you not as you are now, loveliest of creatures, but as a slave among a savage race in a land far and unknown to you now."

"My lord!" cried Viviene.

"But heed my words, sweet lass," he said quickly, taking her hand in his, "I shall always come to your aid and fight to the death any who would harm you."

She leaned to him and he kissed and comforted her. He longed to save his woman from the fate he had seen for her. It was a pain about his heart. He then recalled how, as he had ridden in the wood earlier seeking some solution to his fears for Viviene, the words Lord Asteroth had last spoken to him did echo in his mind . . . "Beware of that which makes man most vulnerable, my lord, for

surely it lies in your path." Raum was sure now that
Asteroth had been speaking of love.

"What are your plans now, my lord?" asked
Lady Le Fey.

"Viviene has told me of an isle of seclusion south
of Shetland. We will go there where it is not likely
that Arthur's knights will hound me. Viviene goes
there from time to time and says all we shall need
to live is there."

"Ah, I do agree with your choice of places and
would urge you to leave at once!" said the queen with
new concern. "Even now I sense one approaching
that longs to claim Lord Raum's life."

The demon warrior closed his eyes for a moment
and then said, "Aye, I feel it too. I guess it to be
that innocent whelp Percival."

"I do not wish for this knight's blood to be shed here,
Lord Raum. The king needs little else for an excuse
to drive me from this land. His patience does grow
thin."

"I understand fully," said Raum standing. He then
turned to Viviene and said, "Come my lady, we must
away before Pervical gains the causeway."

But as is often the case, a lady is not to be rushed
when preparing for a journey. Thus it was that
Percival, upon leaving the forest and approaching
the causeway, saw two riders at its far end coming
from the castle. His young eyes were quite sharp
and he quickly saw that the first was the fiendish
knight on his monstrous horse and the second was
Lady Viviene upon the back of a fine palfrey. Percival
continued onto the causeway but Raum and Lady
Viviene reined in their mounts and sat watching
his approach.

The three met halfway between the castle and

dry land. "I know not how you came to be this foul knight's captive, my lady," said Percival saluting Viviene, "but you may retire back to the castle while I make certain this will be his last ride upon the earth."

"Sir Percival," answered Viviene, "do let us pass. Lord Raum does not hold me against my will for he is my paramour. I give you my word he means no harm to you or the king. We leave this fair land and shall bother you no more."

"You have been damned by your lust, my lady, and your words are tardy. Far too many of our countrymen have died at his hands already. Now do stand aside and let us do manly battle."

"Do as he asks, sweet girl," said Raum in a rumbling voice as he drew his blade.

"Forget not what Merlin did say," cried Viviene.

"What is this?" asked Percival surprised. "You have spoken to Merlin? Where did you see him?"

"He is gone," Viviene stated. "He did appear to us and gave us this warning. If you and Lord Raum did do battle and one were slain, 'twould be the curse of you both for your quests are the same."

"Faw! The hellish knight would not at all seek what I long for," stormed Percival outraged.

"You are an ignorant fellow," said Raum with disgust, "which gives you a marked advantage. What my lady says is true. We must not draw each other's blood. What will it take to satisfy you, stubborn knight?"

"Only your death, vile creature," retorted Percival, his chin jutting in defiance. "If it is in you to ask God's forgiveness, please do so now. I desire the best results with your death for us both."

Raum cursed under his breath and then, raising his

sword skyward, called out words unknown to the young knight. Suddenly the air was filled with screaming ravens pouring from the wooded shore. They swarmed about Sir Percival frightening his mount badly. The beast leaped into the air and spun about causing the startled knight to drop his weapon and hang on to his saddle with both hands. The horse continued to leap and cavort about in its attempt to avoid the enraged birds. Soon the crazed animal's feet slipped from the edge of the causeway and both horse and rider plunged into the murky water and floundered in the gluelike mire.

Raum sat his mount looking down at the slime-covered Percival and said, "In days to come, youthful knight, recall this time when one demon saved your chance to rise to your glorious destiny." He spurred his great charger, as did Lady Viviene her mount, and they rode quickly across the remaining stretch of causeway and vanished in the gloom of Alder Wood.

PART 4

Retribution

S PRING CAME TO THE HILLS of Camelot quietly and was hardly noticed by the people of Arthur's court. Great formations of geese and ducks had passed overhead but were seen only by those who hunted near the lakes. Long before green had shown on any bush or tree, the lusty knights of the Round Table were seen upon the meadow in sporting combat.

Prince Jal, exiled from his homeland in the north, spent much of his time listening to and sorting out information received at court concerning the whereabouts of the notorious demon-knight Raum. There had not been any such information, that could be counted on as reliable, for over two months. The boy prince had grown irritable as time passed, for he became increasingly sure that this cruel knight whom he pursued had somehow escaped him and was no longer in the realm of King Arthur. He had questioned Sir Percival, the last to see Raum, so often that the knight now avoided this royal guest of the king. He had also spent time questioning Lady Morgan Le Fey, the king's sister,

during a call she had made recently at Camelot.
'Twas at her castle that Raum was last seen leaving
with her handmaid Viviene. Morgana, which is what
she insisted Jal call her, had been gracious during
the questioning but not informative. As far as she
could tell the monstrous knight had entered her castle
of Dolorous Garde by killing several of her most
trusted guards, cast a spell upon poor Lady Viviene
and stolen her away. She said she could guess Raum's
whereabouts no more than she could Merlin's,
the vanished court magician that Raum seemed
intent upon locating.

Arthur's queen Guinevere had noticed the visiting
prince's changing mood. She spoke to her husband
of her concern for the boy suggesting Arthur attempt
to interest Jal in some enterprise that would divert
his brooding thoughts.

Thus it was that Jal, at the king's prompting,
began a study of falconry with the court falconer,
Thomas, as his tutor.

Spring broke fully upon the lands of Camelot
the day Thomas took young Jal up into the hills
to hunt and fly their birds.

It seemed all the wild flowers had waited for
this one day to burst forth in a glory of color that
made everyone rejoice in the spirit of spring. Calves,
colts and lambs jumped about on wobbly legs in
the pastures with their mothers.

Jal galloped his horse to a hilltop holding his
padded gauntlet aloft letting the hooded bird ride
with wings outstretched. He had just wheeled about
to signal Thomas, who remained below in the
valley, that he was about to release his falcon.
His attention was quickly drawn, however, to a
rider bursting from the forest and racing to where

Thomas sat his mount. When the rider pulled up
beside Thomas they engaged in talk for a moment
before he resumed his mad ride toward Camelot.
Then the falconer whistled shrilly to Jal indicating
he should return to him immediately. This the boy
did, all curiosity.

"What excites that man so?" asked Jal pulling
abreast of the falconer.

"News, my lord," answered Thomas. "He brings
news most dire from Orkney. Vikings is what has
happened, and many a good man is dead for it. It
seems the bloody heathens have come to that fair isle
to claim it as their own!"

They rode straightaway to the castle and found
the messenger's news had already sparked great
commotion. Everywhere pages ran, squires readied
their knight's livery and armor, knights shouted
orders and made vows to one another while ladies
cried encouragement to their champions. Jal quickly
dismounted, handing his hunting bird to Thomas,
and ran through the milling crowd in the vast
courtyard. All about him was a cacophony of sound.
He heard the neighing of horses being made ready
for travel, the clanking of armor, the excited voices
of people, the hysterical barking of hounds and the
cries of geese about to be trampled.

Jal ran up the stone steps taking three with each
stride. He entered the upper hall and made his
way past scurrying servants and ladies. It was here
that he bumped roughly into a knight stepping into
the passageway from his quarters.

Jal quickly recognized the knight as Sir Gareth.
"Gareth," cried Jal, "what word have you of your
father King Lot?"

"Alas, he is sore wounded and has been brought

from Orkney to Scotland by litter, my prince," said Gareth choking back his tears for this son did love his father the King of Orkney. "I know not if he still lives or is dead."

"Take heart, kind knight," said Prince Jal, "we shall soon be at his side."

"You plan to go with us, my lord?"

"Indeed. I should guess that this assault upon your home isle was not a random choice for the Vikings but one of vengeance. 'Twas there your father and I did scuttle the Norse fleet after its raids at Duncansby and Gavinshire. They lost much and have come with the spring to retaliate. My hand was in at the beginning of this matter and will be in at the end."

"You need feel no guilt for what has befallen Orkney, my prince."

"Feelings of guilt are not what drives me to this adventure, Sir Gareth, but the chance that among these returning Norsemen, I shall find Raum."

"Ah, it follows, my lord," said Gareth clapping a hand on the prince's shoulder. "Very well, I should like you to ride with me and keep me good company so that I do not shame the glory of the Round Table with my tears."

"There is no shame in such tears, worthy knight. I too have lost a father and 'tis this that urges me to battle now."

The serfs and vassals of the countryside came out to cheer the passing army. Seldom had such a spectacle been seen by these backward folk. Before the great assembly rode trumpeters and flag bearers giving full view to Arthur's standard. The king followed with Lancelot, Gawain and Bran. They

were followed by Gareth and Prince Jal. After these
came the other many knights and squires of the
Round Table who were followed in turn by a multi-
tude of men-at-arms, most of which were on foot and
the earth fairly trembled to their marching. Large
drums and drummers mounted on mules sounded
the cadence and these were joined by spirited pipers.
Each knight carried a lance pointed skyward, gaily
colored pennons flying, which gave illusion of a
forest moving over the sun-drenched hills.

As the days passed, the army from Camelot was
joined along the way by those kings of Scotland loyal
to Arthur and by many who were not so friendly
but would assist him in his battle against a common
enemy.

At night large fires were built in the many camps
that stretched over the countryside. Since the nights
were still cold, the men would sit by the fire and
listen to minstrels sing their ballads until they would
nod off to sleep in their blankets. There was some
quarreling among the men, especially between Scots
and Welshmen. Arthur was quick and stern in putting
down such disturbances, warning the men that if
they were to wound any of their fellow warriors he
would take it as an act of treason.

Many days passed before this vast body of fighting
men approached the retreating army of King Lot.
Gareth rode into the camp of the forlorn and defeated
men of Orkney with the young Finnish prince beside
him. Spying one of his father's most trusted knights
Gareth called out to him. The man waved but did
not smile which troubled Gareth greatly. When the
man was finally reached among the sorry and
wounded men, Gareth quickly asked the condition
and whereabouts of his father.

"A short way up this road, my lord, you shall find a hermitage where your father the king does lie in the able care of the wise friar," said the weary knight. "Praise be that your mother was abroad and safe, my lad."

"I thank you, Sir Britt, for your information and kind thoughts," said Gareth. He then turned to find Prince Jal already mounted and eager to ride to the hermitage.

They rode through the greening woods passing many a tired and wounded man along the way. 'Twas not long before they caught sight of the woodland cottage they took to be the hermitage they sought for a lance stood before it bearing the colors of King Lot. The guards at the doorway recognized Sir Gareth and quickly ushered him and Jal into the presence of Lot who lay still and ashen on a cot near the fire. A small man in sandals and habit sat next to him reading from a tattered book of prayers. Seeing the two newcomers, the friar closed his book and stood blessing the knight and his companion.

"I am Gareth and the son of this noble king. How does he fare, good brother?"

"He rests, my lord," said the friar, "and do not fear for the life of this brave man for he shall surely recover to fight another day. Ah, that I could join you on your march northward. I am passing good with a sword, you know, and could deliver many a heathen Viking to holy judgment."

"Your service here is more valued now, dear friar," said Gareth warmly.

"Is that my son?" asked Lot in a rasping voice, his pale eyes slightly open.

" 'Tis I, father, and your friend Prince Jal."

"Ah," sighed the bloodied king, "praise be you

were not there, Prince Jal, for they would have enjoyed catching you. They must surely have informers among our people for they knew of your role in the burning of their ships last autumn."

"How do you know this, noble Lot?" asked Jal.

"We had taken a few captives before we were overwhelmed by the enemy's reinforcements. A few hot irons loosened their tongues. The one who leads this invasion is named Wulfgar and was captain of the raids at Duncansby and Gavinshire. He holds that the responsibility for the destruction of his ships and crews is yours to a great degree."

"Dear friend," said Jal holding the old warrior's hand, "you must rest, I know, but I must ask one last question . . ."

"I heard no mention of the giant knight you seek," said Lot with a choking laugh.

Jal thanked him and rose to his feet. As he stepped into the balmy spring air he breathed deeply in an attempt to disperse his feelings of disappointment.

There were only fifteen longboats and two ships awaiting the army when it reached the coast that faced distant Orkney. Arthur was in a rage of frustration at not having more boats for the crossing to the invaded isle. He rode up and down the beach, his horse's hooves kicking up spray from the shallow surf. He stood in his stirrups as he rode shouting orders and cursing any who moved too slowly.

There had not been any sign of the Nordic invaders as yet. Orkney could just be seen in the distant morning haze. There were not even campfires or smoke to be seen on the island shores nor any signal fires upon its heights. Sir Bran sat his mount and gazed across the water. Beside him was Sir Gawain.

"Could it be they have left?" mused Bran.

"Not likely," replied Gawain. "They are a tricky lot and you will always be better off thinking the worst when dealing with the Vikings."

The king came riding through the surf shouting, "To the boats, you men! The animals go to the ships, men to the boats!"

As the men surged down the beach to the boats, all Britons could have been proud of their bravery and high spirits. Among them ran Gareth and Prince Jal while Gareth's squire led their horses to the nearest ship. Somewhere the piper began to play loudly and someone began singing a song familiar to all that concerned itself with the nobility found in battle.

High above the sea among an outcropping of stone sat Wulfgar and his captains. All showed the marks of recent fighting but all looked eager to engage the fresh troops they knew would soon be sent against them. Wulfgar's fur cloak was blood-soaked as were his leg bindings and even his beard yet he honestly boasted that he had no new wounds upon him. "I am here to bathe in the blood of my enemies," he laughed.

"I think I can see boats coming through the mist," said a young warrior at Wulfgar's side.

"Good, good," rumbled the rotund chieftain, "let them come. Watch closely and make sure Arthur is among those first to land. Watch also for any fitting the description of the boy prince. Are all the men in place, Stegi?"

"They are, my chief," answered the young warrior.

"Remember now," said Wulfgar, "they must all

land and cross over this hill before we signal the fleet and fire our first arrows."

As the men leaped from the boats and waded ashore, Arthur shouted that none proceed until the horses were unloaded from the ships.

"Something does seem wrong here, my king," said Lancelot looking about warily.

"I quite agree," said Arthur, "but without the aid of Merlin's gifted sight we can only press ahead. Yet I do find it strange that the Viking chief would not stay to defend that which he fought so hard to win."

"At least we are safely landed," said Lancelot. "If he attacks us now we will fight on firm ground which is more our way than his."

A squire wearing the royal livery ran forward leading the king's spirited stallion. Soon the knights were all mounted and moving up the rock-crested hill in a sweeping line. Bowmen on foot, and carrying the added weaponry of light spears, followed. As they moved inland the boats and ships moved away from the shore to return and ferry the next wave of fighting men to Orkney.

At a signal from Lancelot two riders separated from the main body and charged up the hill to disappear among the rocks of the crest. Arthur signaled the advance to slow until the two scouts should return with their report. Their wait, however, was in vain for no men showed on the rocks above, neither friend nor enemy. There had been no sound to indicate the scouts had seen or met the Vikings. Arthur chewed the end of his mustache irritably and signaled the men to fan out a little farther. This done he gave the order to charge over the hilltop.

"Stay close!" shouted Gareth to Jal as their horses leaped forward.

The Britons swarmed over the crest in a wave of flashing armor and weapons. No sooner had they began to race downward toward the valley than they sighted the Viking stockade. It lay below them among the trees with high poles from which several bodies swung suspended.

Seeing the tortured victims, Gawain shouted a curse of rage and cried to Arthur, "We must hurry, they may still live!"

The others, including the king, matched his charge down the heather-covered slope until, one after the other, the horses fell with shrill cries of pain as their riders were sent hurtling end over end down the hill.

"Hold!" bellowed Arthur bringing his mount to a halt, but his warning came too late. All but a few of the horses were down with legs broken from the holes Wulfgar's men had dug all along the hillside and then covered with the heather. Most of the fallen riders were either injured or knocked senseless. The men who followed on foot stopped short only to be cut down from behind by a shower of arrows from the Viking archers who sat concealed beneath the large rimrocks they had just passed. The archers now leaped from cover and swarmed down on the fallen knights with swords drawn to finish what their bows had begun.

Waving his shining blade above his head, Arthur called to those still able to fight to go against the archers and try to gain the ridge. Few of the men could understand this order but from his place atop his horse the king could see the great mass of Viking warriors charging up the hill from the cover of the valley trees. It was plain their small band could never stand against such numbers. There was only one small hope left to them.

"Upward, men!" called Arthur. "We must go over the ridge and call our boats back!"

Below them the Norsemen surged upward led by Wulfgar. At his side was his young protegé Stegi. The youthful warrior bayed his war cry like a hound on the scent.

Arthur's horse was having difficulty moving up the rocky hill with any speed. Gawain ran beside the horse and tried to shield it and the king from the enemy flying down upon them but could not. They leaped down from the rocky heights shrieking like banshees and Gawain caught the first to reach him with his spear and vaulted the kicking man overhead and crashing down the slope. The next he met with his sword slicing the man's thick neck almost in half. Arthur hacked and swung his great sword first on one side of his charging mount and then on the other. Great streams of blood arched about him giving testimony to the fine work his blade was doing that day. For one brief second the valiant king saw Gareth and Jal, their backs against a great stone, fighting six of the enemy before being overrun.

Arthur's attention was again drawn to Gawain beside him who was now going to his knees clawing to free himself from the man upon his back. The king's sword flashed downward and with a groan the man rolled from Gawain with a split skull.

"Here," said Arthur reaching a strong hand down to him, "swing up behind me! We are near to the top!" This Gawain did and saw that they were indeed at the summit of the hill. The stallion charged over the crest and down the other side toward the sea,

both men clinging to his back as he twisted and
turned among the fallen rocks.

Suddenly Arthur cried out a great curse and
Gawain looked to see what had caused the king's
outburst. What he saw made him feel weak. The
boats had left the shore and were halfway across
the channel to Scotland but the thing that made
Gawain's heart turn cold was the sight of a large
Viking fleet fast approaching the small boats from
the west.

"Dismount, Gawain," ordered Arthur bringing the
horse to a complete halt. "My place is with my men
back over this hellish ridge. If they are to die at the
hands of the heathens, there is little I may do but die
with them. Save yourself if you can, noble knight, and
return to avenge us another day."

"You speak in haste, my liege," said Gawain
pointing out to sea. "The wind does fail the Viking
sails. Our boats are matching the dragon-ships' pace.
Take heart, my king, for they will gain the shore
before they are joined by the enemy."

"Our two ships," exclaimed Arthur, "they sail into
the path of the Viking ships! They sacrifice their
vessels for they know they could not outdistance the
Norsemen. Their maneuver shall give the boats the
needed time to gain the shore."

Just then a shout rang out behind them and a
great and bloody figure in tattered furs and horned
helmet stood glaring down at them from the rocks
above. He was quickly joined by many others.

"We must away," said Arthur spurring the horse to
a headlong plunge down the hillside toward the sea.
The powerful steed raced along the shore until those
upon the ridge were lost from view.

Sir Kay, awaiting the returning boats so that he could lead the second wave of Arthur's men across the channel, gave orders for all to withdraw, and go to cover, the moment the Viking sails were seen. From tree-covered ravines and clefts they watched their boats lead the enemy to shore. They watched the Britons leap from their boats and run up the shore as the Vikings spilled over the gunwales of the dragon-ships waving their weapons and splashing into the surf. Kay let all the Norse vessels beach before lifting the signal horn to his lips. Two short blasts from this instrument sent the great army surging from cover, much to the horror of the invaders.

The battle did not remain such for long but became a methodical butchering of the Vikings until Sir Percival shouted pleas of mercy for the fallen enemy. So loved was this strange, young knight that at last the Britons began sparing lives as they disarmed the remaining prisoners. Sir Percival rode to where Kay sat his mount surveying the carnage. "Well, Sir Kay," smiled Percival, "we have our ships now."

Wulfgar sat on the large stone cursing as he peered into the mist that had gathered over the water. "This changing weather has betrayed us! Where are the ships? I gave no order for them to land on the mainland. If I find they have, I'll slit someone's throat!" Wulfgar turned to Stegi, who sat among those gathered about the old chieftain, and asked, "Have you any word of their elusive king?"

"We are still searching, my captain."

"Have you taken the prisoners to the valley?"

"We have. Would you care to inspect them now?"

"Not until I see our ships returning," grumbled Wulfgar.

"Odin smiles upon you, Wulfgar," laughed one of the others, "for I see their sails in the haze just now."

"Very well," said the war chief rising and throwing his fur cloak back over his shoulders, "let us go see our catch."

The various Nordic methods of interrogation were well underway when Wulfgar and his company entered the valley stockade. Screams could be heard everywhere and also laughter. They were nearing the stone hut that now served as Wulfgar's field headquarters when young Stegi nudged his chieftain and pointed in the direction of a group of prisoners bound and tethered close to a grove of trees.

"Ah, ah, ah," breathed Wulfgar as he viewed the helpless men. He walked slowly to where the men lay, his eyes shining brightly and fixed on one prisoner in particular. He reached out a thick hand and grasped the blond lad's collar.

The youth's cold blue eyes glared hatred at the Viking chief as he said, "Take your filthy hands from me!"

Wulfgar roared with laughter as he ripped the boy's coat open with one jerk of his hand. There on a gold chain hung the royal emblem of Ever-spring. Still laughing Wulfgar struck the lad's handsome face a resounding blow that sent him pitching, unconscious, into a fellow prisoner.

"My prince!" cried out the other bound man before being silenced by a heavy kick from Wulfgar's foot.

The chieftain then lifted the inert youth in his arms and carried him to where a horse-drawn cart stood near the hut. He threw the boy into the crude vehicle and then turned to Stegi who followed close behind him.

"This is what I came for, Stegi," said Wulfgar. "The other prisoners mean nothing to me. I shall take my prize home and play with him for long hours before I feel kind enough to let him die."

"But there are great personages among those knights captured, my captain," protested Stegi. "One of these is responsible for the deaths of at least twenty of our men. Some say he is the famous Frenchman, Lancelot."

"That matters little to me. Put all the prisoners against the stockade wall and have the archers finish them."

"Some of the village men and farmers, as well as some of their women, are among the captives."

"Kill them, Stegi."

"We could take the women and ransom some of the more noted knights."

"Kill them!" shouted Wulfgar.

"You have told us of the demon warrior Raum," said Stegi not moving away, "and said his savagery was so great that he should never be allowed to return to Norway. Now you act the same as he. Tell me, Wulfgar, what is the difference?"

"You go too far, Stegi," hissed Wulfgar touching the hilt of his sword. "I am still your teacher and chieftain."

"Only so long as you can prove yourself worthy of such titles. You have let your need for vengeance on this whelp of a boy cloud your judgment."

"I'll have your tongue for . . ." began Wulfgar but was cut short by shouting from the ridge. The army of the Britons came down the hills like a great flood. Wulfgar's mouth remained open in disbelief.

Stegi leaped into the cart where Jal lay bound and semiconscious. A poor farm horse stood in the traces. Stegi grabbed the reins and shouted to Wulfgar, "Quick, into the cart! We can make a run for the cove where your ship lies anchored!"

"But we must fight!" shouted the chieftain as he stared dazedly at the advancing waves of armored men and horses.

"There are too many, my captain!" cried Stegi dragging the old warrior onto the cart. He slapped the lines hard across the nag's bony rump and they started through the milling camp which was now in a state of total panic.

Raum had finished building the shelter for the new lambs and gone to the well for a cooling drink when Viviene appeared in the doorway of the cottage. She said nothing, only smiled and watched him. He spilled much of his drink down his bare chest and soaked the leather trousers she had made for him. He set aside the wooden bucket from which he drank and wiped his wide mouth with the back of his hand. As he stood returning the girl's gaze her white teeth flashed into a smile. He too smiled and began walking toward her. She withdrew into the cottage and he quickly followed.

"Have you finished your building so soon, my lord?" she asked in a teasing voice.

His arms were around her now as he answered, "Aye, I've finished and a good thing too, with a woman of your temperment and beauty luring me always from my work."

"Ah, now, my lord," she said with a musical laugh, "you were not compelled to come in to me. I have cast no spell upon you."

"Ah, but you have, loveliest of women," he sighed. "You have cast the one spell I have no defense for. In my realm, love is an unknown emotion and therefore I can do little else but surrender to your unsurpassed charm."

She held his face in her hands for a moment staring intently into his eyes. At last she said softly, "You do change, my lord."

"How so?"

"In many ways," she said suddenly becoming nervous. "Your eyes, as an example, are not the fiery coals they once were. I can now see pupils and irises in them though they still are quite red. Your speech and manner has changed also. Where has my deliciously evil brute gone? You now seem gentler and more . . ."

"Loving," finished Raum for her. "I could say the same of you, sweet girl. Where once your only pleasure came from inflicting your will and pain upon others, you now are concerned with my needs and my pleasure more than your own. I have watched you tending the ewes and lambs and you are all tenderness. Do not resist this change, my sweet, for it is right and how wonderful to change together. I find these changes in you the crowning glory of your flawless beauty."

"But when you are not here it frightens me," she whispered before he kissed her. They held each other tightly for a very long while.

It was late one afternoon when Raum finished damming a small stream in the meadow to catch water for the sheep. He stood and stretched his muscled back and arms in the warmth of the sun. The ravens stirred themselves from a nearby oak and flew overhead casting their dark shadows across him. He suddenly seemed chilled. Noticing the dirt that caked his hands, he went to the brook and stripped out of his clothes. He then plunged into the water almost crying out against its frigid temperature. He could not say why, but he was obsessed with washing himself clean as never before. When he had finished scrubbing himself, he dipped water in his hands to rinse his face. Suddenly he became motionless peering into his cupped hands. There in the water he held was the face of Prince Jal. The blond lad's face seemed pained and his lips parted but no sound came.

The vision quickly vanished and Raum heard laughter from the water of the stream. In the rippling current appeared the image of his old superior in Netherworld, Lord Asteroth. Raum turned his back to the image and rinsed his face as he had first intended.

"Are you trying to wash my face from your memory, Lord Raum, or is it the boy's you wish to be rid of?" laughed Asteroth.

"I find neither face particularly interesting," said Raum stepping from the water and walking to the grassy knoll where his clothes lay.

"The change in you does fascinate me," said the powerful demon ruler. "Your skin still is dark but now takes on a rosy blush. Perhaps it is the witch you have as company that does this to you."

"Lady Viviene is a part of the change I pass through, not the cause of it," retorted Raum.

"And what do you think causes your transformation?" asked Asteroth in a shrill and mocking voice.

"Mine own will, my lord," replied Raum pulling on his big boots. "I will myself to change."

"Truly amazing," said Asteroth, "but why do you do this thing?"

"I no longer wish to be confined to Netherworld with its limiting atmosphere to growth and experience. I desire to move through higher planes and spheres of being."

When Asteroth finally spoke Raum thought he detected a note of fear in the hateful voice. "How came you by such thoughts? Who told you of planes other than those of Netherworld, the last of which is this one peopled by the Mabden?"

"None told me, my lord," said Raum lifting his digging tools to his broad shoulder, "I just found myself thinking of it and could not dismiss it from my mind. It was as though I had always known it. I will say further, Lord Asteroth, that after seeing my change and hearing my words, you shall have enough cause to doubt your own convictions so that you may never again be fully content. This is the curse that comes with the blessing of knowledge. If in truth you did not know of these higher planes, you shall not be able to ignore the possibility of their existence now." He turned to leave.

"How dare you!" screamed Asteroth, clouds of steam now rising from the brook. "Of course I know there is a plane above that of the Mabden. It is the realm of the Maker and is unfit for all save Him. You are a fool!"

Raum glanced back at the fuming image and asked, "Have you not wondered that if the Maker created us why it is we are not fit for life on His plane? I do not doubt this to be the case, Lord Asteroth, but what if we were, in truth, created in His realm first and then decended into Netherworld? One might say then that the higher planes are not entirely alien to man or demon. Is it not a fascinating idea, my lord?"

"'Tis obvious your change has brought insanity!"

"Have you wondered, my lord," continued Raum, "where those who die but do not come to Netherworld might go?"

"Of course, idiot, son of a thousand idiots! They simply cease to exist!"

"Does not the over-simplicity of your answer trouble you? I contend there are several planes between that of the Maker and the Mabden just as there are between the Mabden and Netherworld. I do intend to travel these higher planes," said Raum without emotion.

"And by what means do you intend to achieve this foolish goal?"

"I . . . I cannot say with certainty. I do feel, however, it will come by way of an emotion you and those of Netherworld know little of. As you know I speak of the emotion termed love."

"Ah, love!" cried Asteroth. "So you have indeed become mortal! You are wrong, of course, in saying we of Netherworld know nothing of love. We mate and have our sexual recreations as you well know. We do not, however, involve ourselves in the other foolish emotions that these Mabden seem so given to."

"If you refer to sacrifice, kindness and unselfishness, I would say you have thrown out the better part of love," replied Raum.

Asteroth laughed uproariously and said, "How can you hope to travel this road of selfless love when you reflect back upon the things you have done just since entering this world of mortality?"

Raum's face took on something of its former evil

countenance. "Why did you show me Prince Jal's face in the water?" he asked.

"Ah yes," purred Asteroth, "there is an unpleasant memory for you, is it not? Well, I must confess I did not have that in mind when showing you the boy's image. My only wish was that you be kept abreast of what is happening about you."

"Stop your game playing and explain fully or I shall leave you babbling with the water."

"You were never known to be a patient demon, Lord Raum. Very well, I shall tell you of the situation your former victim now finds himself in. Prince Jal is the prisoner of the very Viking captain who brought you to these shores."

"Wulfgar! How did this happen?"

"Yes, I do believe that is his name," continued Asteroth. "He invaded Orkney, you know. . . . Oh, you didn't? You must stay in better touch with your fellow mortals, my lord. Yes, he landed in Orkney for the prime purpose of luring Arthur and the prince into his trap. It is unfortunate that the weather turned treacherous to the Viking chief and Arthur did escape him but not so the boy. Old Wulfgar now has the boy on his ship sailing for Norway where he will make the lad suffer for weeks before killing him. All this comes from your bringing these two lives together, Lord Raum. How does this fit into your scheme to gain entry into the realm of love and kindness?"

The shrill laughter from the demon ruler echoed in Raum's ears as he turned and walked away through the field of wildflowers.

"Why must you leave," sobbed Viviene, "when you

say you are happier here with me, my lord? I do not understand."

He fastened the heavy sword in its scabbard to his belt. He then turned to her saying, "My leaving brings me pain unlike any I have felt. A knife in my heart would be pleasanter. Yet I must go. I must attempt to undo some of what I've done."

"But that hateful boy only hopes to slay you. Why then do you go to his aid?"

"The responsibility is mine," he said quietly as he came to her and lifted her in his arms. "I can never explain it so that you would be satisfied, my girl. Know only that I must do this thing and know also that I do love you more than any other."

She nestled against him crying and he made no move to leave until at last her sobs became less frequent. He then bowed his head and kissed her cheek.

"I love you so, my lord," she whispered. "I no longer want the life I had before. I want only you, here with me on our little isle."

"Then stay here and wait for me, sweet Viviene. I'll not be gone longer than is necessary."

She walked with him to the door but no farther. After a last embrace he stepped through the portal and she closed the door after him. Slowly she went to her knees and gave herself up to the heartache and loss that she felt.

When Raum rode his big charger onto the waiting boat he spoke not a word to the ferryman, who was a trusted friend of long standing to Viviene. When they reached the coast, the sinister knight dropped a pouch of gold into the man's hand and rode ashore.

Wulfgar lounged on a bench near the central fire in his great hall. A heavy but handsome woman sat on the floor beside him feeding him strips of fish from a dish she held. Stegi entered unannounced causing the old chieftain to wave the woman hurriedly from the hall.

"I hope you are feeling well, my captain," greeted the young warrior.

"I do."

"And the prisoner, how does it go with him? Is he still amusing you?"

"Yes."

"Then I take it he is not dead," smiled Stegi. "We have been home many days now and I feared you might be tiring of your sport with the boy."

"Oh, no," said Wulfgar, "I enjoy his company much more than I do yours, friend Stegi."

"I had hoped we could resolve the bad feelings between us, my chieftain," said Stegi ruefully. "That is the purpose of my coming here this morning. I came to tell you I have been wrong. When the army of Britons attacked us at Orkney, you were the bravest one there. I showed my weakness when I made you flee with me."

"It will not help for us to lie to one another," said Wulfgar. "If I had not been willing to leave the battle you could not have forced me. You give yourself far too much credit. You are right only in the fact that you are wrong," laughed the old warrior cynically. "I am still the best leader you shall find anywhere in Norway or Sweden."

"I no longer doubt this," said Stegi quietly. "That is why I must tell you what I have heard."

"Then speak."

"As you know, captain, these last two adventures in Briton land have cost us dearly. Few men have returned. The absence of a strong fighting force at home does trouble me as I'm sure it does you."

"Wrong again, Stegi. I fear nothing here in Norway. Now get to your first purpose, as you said you would. What is it you have heard?"

"A ship was seen leaving a remote fjord to the south. Its markings were Danish and two of our ships overtook it. Once stopped, its captain told a most interesting story. It seems a gigantic knight with a monstrous black stallion bought passage for Norway on his ship. The knight instructed him on where to put in. After landing the knight rode off into the forest but the captain could not say in which direction."

Wulfgar's face was pale now. He kicked a log onto the fire and said, "There is no bad blood between the demon and me. Let him come. He probably wants to watch the boy die. We'll grant him that and then he shall leave Norway."

"But you did forbid him to come here!"

"Again you are wrong! I said only that I would not transport him here."

"That might be insult enough to . . ."

"Silence!" shouted Wulfgar, his hand going to his sword.

"Take care, Wulfgar, for it is hate that has made you act without thought before. Do not let it guide you now. Hate is a destroyer! You must put it aside."

"What kind of nonsense are you spouting now? Who told you such things?"

"A German. He is newly come to Norway and is traveling about speaking to the people."

"How did he come by such ideas?"

"He has a book that contains the words of the

Christian God. This is where such ideas are found."

"A Christian! I should have known! Why haven't the people killed him? Odin will bring a curse upon our land if we listen to this other God."

Wulfgar was in such a rage that he raised his broad blade above Stegi, ordering him out of his lodge. The young man left shaking his head in dismay.

No sooner had Stegi stepped from the great hall than he became aware of some excitement in the village below. He then saw a cloud of ravens coming from the forest and recalled Wulfgar's mentioning the strange relationship these winged death symbols had with the demon-knight. Stegi spun about and ran into the hall shouting, "He comes! He comes!"

"I know, stupid lout!" thundered Wulfgar standing by the fire, sword still in hand. "I knew he was here before you left. Can you not hear those cursed birds?"

The towering knight rode through the narrow village streets speaking to no one nor was he spoken to. A band of people that looked quite war weary and in ill health followed behind the big charger. After dismounting before Wulfgar's great lodge, Raum tethered his mount to a large pine that grew near the building and strode to the unguarded doorway where he entered.

Both Wulfgar and Stegi stood facing him with drawn swords.

"Greetings, old friend," said Wulfgar loudly.

"Greetings, Wulfgar," replied Raum, "do I interrupt some argument?"

"No, no, friend Raum," laughed Wulfgar quickly,

"I am just teaching my pupil Stegi a few fine points of swordsmanship."

"I would enjoy seeing this," said Raum, "do continue."

"We have finished," said Stegi, his face flushed to a bright crimson.

"Indeed we have," chuckled Wulfgar, "but perhaps another time, my lord, though I'm sure there is little I can teach you about swordplay. Now please tell me what brings you to my land."

"You have captured the Finnish boy who hunts me and hopes to avenge his father's death."

"So?"

"I would have you turn him over to me so that we might go off alone and settle our differences."

"What?" exclaimed Wulfgar. "You are speaking of the one who caused the burning of our fleet at Orkney and the deaths of many a gallant Viking!"

"If you know that, you must also know that it was I who caused him to do this thing. The boy is so filled with hate for me that he thinks of no one else."

Stegi shot a quick look of triumph at Wulfgar but the old warrior did not acknowledge it.

"I could never let the puny lad go," said Wulfgar firmly. "I have spent all winter dreaming of teaching him to mind his own affairs. You shall not have him."

"Even you will admit, old friend," said Raum with his evil smile, "that I would be the worst thing that could come the boy's way. If you truly wish to punish him, let me have him."

"Listen to him, my leader," pleaded the young Viking. "You have had your pleasure with the boy. Now watch the horror in his eyes when you give him to Lord Raum."

"It does make for a pretty picture," mused Wulfgar stroking his beard. He walked around Raum eyeing the dark giant. Raum did not turn as Wulfgar paused behind him. The demon's red eyes narrowed as he sensed Wulfgar's movement.

"No!" cried Stegi leaping forward to stop Wulfgar's treacherous thrust at Raum's unprotected back. But Raum was suddenly to one side and the old Viking's lunge passed its target and it was Stegi's cry of agony that brought an end to all movements. Wulfgar's blade had gone deep between the young man's ribs. All three warriors gazed dumbly at the blood gushing from Stegi's side.

Wulfgar was the first to act. He dropped his sword and caught the wounded man in his arms. He then lowered Stegi to a lying position on the floor. "Foolish, foolish Stegi," breathed the chieftain with pain-filled eyes.

"Ah, my captain," choked Stegi in a near whisper, "I know 'twas not you who thrust the blade but hate itself."

"Yes, yes," murmured Wulfgar with bowed head.

"I have no family, my captain, and I fear none shall remember that I was here. Would you build up a cairn of stones for me and fix my name on it?"

"Yes, yes, foolish lad," gasped Wulfgar.

Raum sheathed the blade he had drawn and stepped forward.

"Get back!" bellowed Wulfgar. "This good lad shall not have your face as his last memory of life!"

"He is already dead," said Raum coldly.

Wulfgar sent forth a great moan and hugged Stegi's lifeless body to him.

"Where do you keep Prince Jal?" demanded Raum.

"He is beneath the floor of the storehouse," spat Wulfgar. "Take him and go. Never let me see your terrible face again!"

Prince Jal was unconscious when Raum broke the lock on the trapdoor leading to the cell beneath the storehouse floor. Although none of the Norse villagers assisted him in taking charge of their prisoner, neither did they resist him.

He emerged with the boy across his shoulders and then, after mounting the big horse, held the prince in front of him. They rode this way for some time before Raum halted the stallion in a grove near a stream. He fetched a drink in his hands, letting the water spill over the boy's lips. Jal soon showed signs of awakening. The dark knight put more water on the youth's forehead.

Jal gave a startled cry when he saw Raum's demonic features before him. The knight only laughed and said, "Do not fear, my prince, you are not yet in Netherworld. From your looks, however, I should guess you were not far from it. How long has it been since you ate last?"

"I . . . I've lost all sense of time. I am very hungry . . ."

"I'll get some dried fish from my bags."

"Are you going to kill me?" Jal asked sleepily.

"That was not my plan," replied Raum returning to him and offering him some fish. "I have grown sick of the events and consequences caused by my first days in this world of yours. 'Tis my plan to do what I might in payment for the hardships I have caused."

"And how do you propose to restore life to my father?" the old anger showing in Jal's weakened voice.

"Ah, already you show signs of being your old self. Good. I shall get you a horse to ride and we shall return to your home at Ever-springs and to your mother Queen Gudren."

"Then you do not know?" asked the youth as he searched the knight's face for the truth. "My mother is in a village to the north and very far from here. The quake that closed our fjord also caused our land to flood until all Ever-spring was below the steaming water."

"Ah, I did not know!" sighed the giant closing his fiery eyes. "Would . . . can you ever . . . ever, my prince . . ."

"Lord Raum!" exclaimed the boy. "Are you trying to ask my forgiveness? What trick is this?"

The knight turned away from Jal saying, "Much has happened since first we met. I did find the magician and much more."

"He answered your questions?"

"Aye, he did but not as clearly as I would have liked. One of the few things I understood in what he said was that I am doomed to a very hard struggle while others may achieve the same goal in a single lifetime."

"What is this mysterious goal and what must you do to reach it?"

"Helping you is one way, perhaps," said Raum quietly, "though Merlin did not say this. My goal is to travel the higher spheres and to do this I have my very inexperienced sense of right to guide me."

"So Merlin put you up to this change of heart, did he?" laughed Jal cynically. "Well, I shall never believe a demon can ever be anything other than a demon."

Raum became quiet for a moment, his eyes glowing brighter with each heavy breath he took. At last he spoke and his voice was like the crack of a whip. "You have played the righteous judge far too long, spoiled brat! I should like to tell you of a man I knew once. He was a good man by your standard of laws and virtues. He was a hard worker and did his job well. He loved a good fight but always kept his sense of fairness. He refused to hold a captive woman in bondage though it was his right. He befriended a boy from his enemy's camp when the boy was fatherless. He grew to love this boy as a son. The boy rewarded this finest of men by filling his helpless body with arrows!"

"Stop it!" screamed Jal rolling over and covering his eyes in the crook of his arms.

"If there is any in this business who must share with me the guilt for the great evil that has been done, it is you, my lad, it is you!"

Weeks passed before Jal rode his bay pony across the Jamtland border and caught sight of the little towers of Bergenklas. He found himself yearning to continue north into that region of Norway now called Finmark for it is peopled now as it was then by a Finnish race of people. It was here that Thorkuld's kingdom lay at Ever-spring.

Prince Jal's thoughts were interrupted by the shouting of the villagers rushing out to meet him. Seeing this reception, the prince was glad Raum had chosen not to accompany him here. The knight rode with the boy until the sea and the Viking kings were far behind. He then gave Jal the following instructions: "Go on to your mother and people. Tell them that their place is in their own land and that they must return to Ever-spring. Lead them back, Prince Jal, and establish your kingdom once again. As for the valley, it shall be ready to welcome you home." With that said the armored warrior charged away through the forest leaving the boy more than a little perplexed.

But Jal had little else he could do other than return to Bergenklas and Stanfel's home where his mother, the queen, still waited for him. There would be someone else awaiting his return also. The memory of warm, fragrant Helga brought a smile to the boy's thin face. His face had not just become thin, but looked much older now after his experiences at the hands of the Vikings. He realized also that soon he would be celebrating his fourteenth birthday.

The village mayor ran out to greet Jal open-armed, coat and scarf flying. "My prince, you have returned to us! Welcome, welcome!"

"Thank you, kind Stanfel," said Jal dismounting, "and how is my mother?"

"She is quite well, dear boy, and will be even better when she sees you."

Jal declined Stanfel's offer of a public banquet in his honor and asked that his first evening meal be with his mother, Stanfel and Helga. The mayor quickly granted the boy's request.

Queen Gudren greeted her son with tears of relief. He spent most of the afternoon relating his experiences to her in her room. When he described his last meeting with Raum, she became deeply thoughtful. After a while she sighed and said, "We should do as the demon said. If his desire was to slay us he could have accomplished this long ago. We have nothing but our poor lives to lose. We should return to Ever-spring."

"I quite agree," smiled Jal.

That evening at table Jal answered Stanfel's and Helga's many questions for an hour then, turning his full attention to the girl, said, "My mother and I have decided to return with our people to our homeland. There is some chance that it is no longer flooded."

"Many of your people have moved on," said Stanfel. "Would it not be simpler for you to settle here with us?"

"Here my mother and I are just homeless refugees, but in Ever-spring she is a queen and I a prince. Better a prince to few than a beggar to all."

"I see your point, proud lad," smiled Stanfel.

"And I do hope to take your daughter with me as my wife, if she and you be agreeable."

Helga blushed glowingly and lowered her bright blue eyes. Stanfel just sat back in his chair staring open-mouthed at Prince Jal.

"My son," said Gudren, "you are very young for such a step. Even among our people, who are known to marry very young, the groom is usually in his sixteenth summer. I do love this girl you have picked, but as a mother and as a queen, I would caution you both."

"My age in experience far surpasses my years, Mother," replied Jal, "and I have matured greatly even these past few weeks. Perhaps I should say that my hated enemy Raum has taught me much in the way of becoming a man of responsibility.

ate does play strange tricks on us. I love Helga and want her as my wife. You shall rule Ever-spring until my sixteenth birthday. 'Tis then I should become king but if I have erred in any way, dear Mother, I vow to step away from the throne and to seat any on it of your choosing."

"Done!" said the queen with a broad smile.

"Done!" echoed Stanfel, gleefully filling everyone's wineglass. He then held his own high and pronounced his toast. "To Helga and Jal and their new life in Ever-spring. May all their babies be fat and healthy."

Had anyone been there to see him, they would have said the demon warrior did grow in size as he stood on the rocky craig facing the fallen mountain where once had been the great fjord. He stretched both his powerful arms outward and shouted his incantation. A green nimbus gathered about him as he continued to roar forth his magical command. The sky darkened rapidly with angry clouds and a fierce wind raced in from the sea sweeping the calling ravens from the air above. A heavy but distant rumble could be heard causing the great horse, Eligor, to cry out and bolt from where he had been left on the beach below. The monstrous stallion galloped away as the surf grew into a thundering rage.

The giant's eyes glowed a brilliant red, his features losing all the softness that had been there a few short weeks earlier. His mouth opened and emitted a high earsplitting sound. This sound continued as the tempest reached full force and lashed the towering demon. It was then the first crack appeared among the huge boulders and streams of water shot through into the howling wind. These were quickly followed by others as Raum's ear-shattering wail continued. Suddenly the

whole earth seemed to heave a great sigh and the dam across the fjord was no more. The boulders and earth came down in a deafening roar followed by a wall of water, ice and steam.

The crag upon which Raum stood joined the falling earth and the warrior of Netherworld fell twisting into the roaring chaos below.

By midnight the moon shone brightly on the now-untroubled tide along the rocky shore. The surf tossed timber and debris upon the beach from time to time and it was in such a mass of torn timber that Raum found himself. The pain about his middle was severe but it kept him from fainting and losing his grip on the logs.

In the moonlight he could see the shore and knew that his raft of tangled pine was drifting in that direction. He had just started to experience a sense of relief when the floating trees which supported him caught some of their branches among rocks hidden below the water's surface. Raum cursed to himself as he gauged the distance to shore. He knew that with the pain, from what he guessed to be cracked ribs, he would never reach the shore before succumbing to his agony and drowning.

As he lay among the twisted branches, he could feel the debris gradually coming apart beneath him. He could only lay there awaiting the inevitable. He suddenly became aware of a familiar sound upon the distant beach. It was the thunderous pounding of hooves upon sand and rock.

"Eligor!" shouted Raum causing almost blinding pain in his chest. A shrill neighing answered from the shore. "Eligor!" called Raum. From the loud splashing sounds, Raum knew the beast had plunged into the waves. "Eligor!" he called and released his hold on the logs.

Spring deepened into the greenness of summer as Raum rested at the ruined castle, doing only the most minor repairs to occupy himself while his injuries healed. He marveled at how fast the grass began to show after a winter spent underwater. Perhaps the warm temperatures of these waters was what had saved the blessed grass. He noted also that there was more pastureland now in Ever-spring for as the valley had filled with its heated flood, the ice along the higher slopes was melted away. Now the water had gone back to its original level leaving beautiful meadows where once had been glacial ice. He had found many abandoned boats high up the mountain side where, when left, they had been moored at water's edge. He used Eligor to drag them down to the lake.

Raum's physical pains did not trouble him half so much as his longing to return to Viviene and their little island in the Hebrides. His anguish was compounded by his growing awareness that his supernatural powers were ebbing. It was only on occasion now, and seldom at will, that he could see the future with any clarity. He felt his inability to communicate mentally with his lady was a part of his general change to mortality. But he had received thoughts from Morgan Le Fey and Nimue, so why not Viviene? He had learned nothing of Viviene from the thoughts of the other ladies for they were filled only with schemes and plots that did not concern him. He had lost his mental contact with Viviene upon reaching the Danish shores. Suddenly he had received only the impression of darkness and silence when trying to contact her.

As soon as he was fit he would leave Ever-spring and

journey back to the little isle regardless of whether or not Gudren and Jal had arrived.

The sturdy deer with their riders formed a slow-moving caravan through the deep snow that never seemed to melt. Here the only difference between summer and winter was the number of hours of daylight. Jal rode his bay and led a line of fine horses he intended to breed if they survived the journey. The success of this venture also depended upon the valley no longer being flooded. The queen and Helga rode together on the backs of two white reindeer, bundled against the painful cold in heavy furs. There were only about forty people in the party but Jal felt sure many more would return once they learned that Ever-spring was reborn to its former state.

A group of young Swedes had joined their party in Bergenklas at Stanfel's recommendation. They were mostly tall, robust men who were looking for a new life since their village had been all but destroyed in a war among the Viking kings. Jal noted with satisfaction that the girls of Ever-spring found the young Swedes quite pleasing and welcomed them into their society. Both Prince Jal and Queen Gudren saw a new beginning for a new Ever-spring; there was no sense in dreaming of the past. It would not be as it was before; it could not be for Thorkuld was dead. Jal, along with the queen, vowed to make the future even greater for Ever-spring than the past had been.

A man riding just ahead of Jal stopped his mount on the rim of the snow crest before them. He wheeled about shouting to Jal and the others. They quickly joined him and saw the enormous green valley spread far below them. Gudren wept as she gazed at its beauty.

"The grass is coming back!" said Jal.

"That is true but we shall have to plant trees," said one of the Swedes. "Ah, we can do it, my prince. Let us plant fruit trees. The warmth of this valley is perfect for such trees!"

"We shall have plenty of time to lay our plans," laughed Gudren, "so let us proceed out of this cold and into our beloved kingdom."

Raum stood in the courtyard adjusting the huge horse's saddle. He looked up from time to time noting the progress of the caravan descending the slopes above. The band was pitifully small and Raum again felt remorse for his part in the fate that had befallen these people. It was this feeling of regret that had prompted him to do all he could for them. It was these feelings also that urged him on his way now that he was sure Jal and Queen Gudren were safely home. He swung his weight up into the saddle and rode from the confines of the castle.

Queen Gudren's sharp eyes picked out the lone horseman riding across the valley below causing her to call her son to her. As Prince Jal rode his pony up beside her, she halted her reindeer and said pointing, "Look there, my son. Only one knight sits his mount so tall. He leaves us without our thanks. Please ride to him and tell him he is welcome to stay with us. It fast becomes apparent that demons, like men, can change."

With a broad smile he urged his bay to race down the mountainside. He rode over the slopes without stopping, across the streams, past the looming castle along the lake's shore where the dark knight was now riding.

Raum heard the prince's shout and slowed his mount to a leisurely trot but did not look back. Soon Jal's horse came galloping up beside him.

"Where are you going, Lord Raum?" asked the boy, breathless.

"There is someone dear to me that awaits my return. I must delay no longer."

"A lady?" asked Jal with enthusiasm. "I, too, have a lady, my lord. We married at Bergenklas. I would have you meet her! The queen wishes to thank you and to invite you to stay with us for a time. For these reasons you must not leave us."

Raum stared at the blond youth in disbelief. "How can you invite me to your hospitality after all that has happened?"

"That is past, Lord Raum. Are we not all beginning afresh this day?"

"Give my highest regards to Queen Gudren and your bride. If you tell them it is a matter of the heart that takes me away, they will surely understand for they, being nature's gentle creatures, know well the ways of love." His eyes moved over the landscape of Everspring. "You will have much work to do in restoring your beautiful kingdom, my prince, and will have cause to buy and trade with merchants for those things you lack. I have left a room filled with new gold below the castle's main tower. I would caution you to not let knowledge of this gold go beyond these mountains for it would bring the Viking hordes upon you for sure."

"But, my lord, how did you come by this wealth?" asked the startled prince.

"Gold is not the precious thing in Netherworld as it is here," laughed Raum. "We make it at will and with little effort. There are even a few men of your world who have done this. Ask no more questions, my prince, and take the gold as payment for some of that which I did destroy. It is my regret that there is much that cannot be so lightly repaid."

"Dwell not on the past, my lord. Know that no matter where your travels lead you there will always be a haven for you here at Ever-spring."

"I would be greatly honored to count you as a friend, Jal," said Raum, obviously touched by the boy's open forgiveness. Perhaps these things came easier to one who was in love.

"Then do count me as a friend, gallant knight, and may your troubles be over now. I pray you do achieve your goal, though I do not pretend to understand it."

The giant warrior took the boy's hand in a firm grip and the two stared into each other's eyes for a moment. Raum then wheeled his great horse about and rode from the valley.

The campfire warmed Raum as he sat eating the hare he had caught and roasted. The big stallion Eligor called softly to him from the darkness where he was tethered. Raum sipped a little wine and leaned back against a massive fir's trunk. He was at peace for, perhaps, the first time since entering this strange and beautiful world of the Mabden.

His eyes were closed and his thoughts were on Viviene when a familiar laugh came from the dancing flames. Raum opened his eyes a little and said without concern, "Greetings, Lord Asteroth, you should have come earlier and dined with me."

"You do seem in an easy mood this evening," said Asteroth's flickering image.

"I am, my lord, but please tell me why you appear before me for you know that you, above all others, bore me most."

Asteroth laughed shrilly and said, "you do amuse me, Lord Raum. To show my goodwill and gratitude for your entertaining ways, I shall answer you promptly. I come to ask if you are returning to your witch-lady?"

Raum's eyes were fully open now. "What of Viviene?"

"I would guess you have found it difficult to reach her mentally," mused Asteroth. "I feel it my duty as your friend and advisor to . . ."

"Is she dead?" snapped Raum.

"Oh, no, my happy and carefree knight. She lives but is not aware of it due to a severe blow she received on her pretty head."

"She is unconscious? Who struck this blow?"

"You would not know him, dear Raum, but your old friend Wulfgar might. The man's name is Bjarni Ax Thrower and he is a ruthless fellow from Iceland. Wulfgar sailed with him on raids to the south."

"How did he find Viviene?"

"He and his crew were raiding along the Welsh coast. They put in at your little island in the Hebrides for rest and water. Spying your lovely lady, Bjarni quickly pursued her. She did resist him but before she could place some hideous curse upon him, he had clubbed her. She is awake now, mind you, but serves him in the simplest of ways for she seems to have the mind of a child and no memory at all."

"Oh, you do enjoy this greatly, don't you, Asteroth?" shouted Raum.

"If I must be honest I must confess to finding a certain pleasure in being your messenger, dear Raum."

"Where is Viviene now, viper's tongue?"

"Why, in Iceland, of course . . . but not for long, I fear. It seems Bjarni is not well thought of there. He and your lady shall be sailing soon for the colonies in Greenland."

"Then I shall go straightaway to Greenland!"

"You may also forget Greenland, my lord," laughed Asteroth, "for their stay there shall be a short one also. It is likely that Bjarni and the senseless girl will have set sail with Leif's foolish fleet for the vast land he calls Vinland."

"The land of the red savages!" cried Raum. "Now I understand the dreadful vision I was shown of my beloved Viviene among a strange savage race far away."

"Ah yes," chuckled Asteroth, "that could be the red race. They might even be able to teach your blood-thirsty lady something new about cruelty and torture."

"Silence, damned slime-mouth!" shouted Raum. "Know that it makes no difference where he takes her. I shall follow and overtake them. If she lives when I reach them, I shall give him a swift death. If she is dead, I shall eat his heart while he still lives!"

"Now that is my old Raum," said Asteroth gleefully. "I can see your demonic ways, with your venomous blood, surging through your veins. In no time at all you shall be just as you once were."

"Pray that I never reach such a state, my lord," hissed Raum through clenched teeth, "for I shall surely come to Netherworld and deal with you as no one has ever dared before!"

Asteroth's laughter ceased as he glared his hatred from the fire. Suddenly the burning logs exploded in a shower of flaming debris and sparks. Asteroth was gone.

Raum stumbled through the darkness to his excited stallion. "There, there, Eligor," he murmured stroking the animal's thick neck. "How would you like to be the first of your kind to see the new continent of Vinland?" He leaned heavily against the great beast and looked up at the moon that was breaking through the flying clouds. Somewhere a raven called mournfully. "Oh, Viviene, Viviene, do be brave. I shall come for you, my lady. This be my troth!" The first tears the demon-knight had ever experienced wove their way down his angular cheeks, yet he was unaware of their presence.

AVON ⬥ MEANS THE BEST IN FANTASY AND SCIENCE FICTION

URSULA K. LE GUIN

The Lathe of Heaven	25338	1.25
The Dispossessed	24885	1.75

ISAAC ASIMOV

Foundation	29579	1.50
Foundation and Empire	30627	1.50
Second Foundation	29280	1.50
The Foundation Trilogy (Large Format)	26930	4.95

ROGER ZELAZNY

Doorways in the Sand	32086	1.50
Creatures of Light and Darkness	27821	1.25
Lord of Light	33985	1.75
The Doors of His Face, The Lamps of His Mouth	18846	1.25
The Guns of Avalon	31112	1.50
Nine Princes in Amber	27664	1.25
Sign of the Unicorn	30973	1.50
The Hand of Oberon	33324	1.50